# CONTENTS

# MOONS OVER TERRA

Based on the screenplay by Rick James

## R.J. HAROLD

PAGE
CHRONICLES
LTD

**Moons Over Terra**

Copyright 2026 by R.J. Harold

ISBN: 979-8-218-01549-0 (Paperback)

Page Chronicles LTD

# CHAPTER ONE

Kyle was ready for anything. His best friends, Mary, Kate and Ethan, were with him, and they all stood in fighting positions waiting for him to give the signal. They always had his back.

The day was gloomy, but the clearing in front of them was a beautiful green field. He saw King Warren across the field mounted on a large black horse. The older man's regal robes and flowing gray beard surprised Kyle. He had expected someone more frightening than a wizard who closely resembled Gandalf the Grey from Lord of the Rings.

But Kyle knew that looks were usually deceiving, and King Warren was evil to his core.

The hundreds of soldiers lined up behind King Warren were more intimidating looking than King Warren. They wore dark armor and helmets with masks, so Kyle couldn't see any of their faces.

That wasn't good.

"We're badly out-numbered here, Ethan," Kyle said. "Can you do anything about that?" He watched Ethan draw words in the air with his finger. Fiery letters spelled out, "We need more soldiers."

Seconds before the last letter faded, hundreds of packs of fierce wolves appeared around their small group. The wolves were all wearing padded protective gear. Several prides of roaring tigers similarly garbed as the wolves appeared and formed a semi-circle around them all.

Kyle shouted a battle cry and charged across the clearing. He knew that his friends and their magical gifts were following behind him. The four-legged animals out-paced them running toward King Warren's army.

Arrows flew from the King's archers spearing several of the animals. Kate threw her cape around their group as a shield and they kept running, advancing on the enemy army.

A flaming bomb from one of the enemy catapults landed within a few feet of Kate. Kyle slashed it with his sword and it broke into thousands of tiny icicles, all shattering on the ground.

Ethan spoke into his crystal ball and a brilliant bright light poured out of it, blinding the front lines of enemy soldiers, giving Kyle the opportunity he needed to draw his sword of fire and ice, freezing some and roasting others while they couldn't see.

More enemy soldiers kept advancing, and Kyle could feel his small group weakening. Kate was showing the strain and her battered cape wouldn't hold much longer, especially while she fought with her sword at the same time.

He was helpless to keep up with all the burning boulders crashing down and exploding the earth around their group. Kyle watched in horror as the sky went dark and lightning flashed, striking Kate's cape.

Kate dropped to the ground, and the cape fell, exposing the group to the onslaught.

Kyle charged the enemy lines, slashing with his sword freezing and burning as many soldiers and he could. The wolves and tigers flanked him, giving him the protection he needed to buy time for his friends to run for cover.

Victory was close.

But as soon as that thought crossed his mind, another bolt of lightening struck.

And his world disappeared.

# CHAPTER TWO

Kyle jerked awake, his breathing heavy.

He checked to make sure his body wasn't full of arrows, or scorched by lightening. He searched his surroundings, momentarily confused about where he was.

He calmed down considerably when he recognized the blue-green walls and his <u>Moons Over Terra</u> video game posters. He had never been so relieved to see the three moons glowing over the green landscape that advertised the imaginary world where he interacted with his friends every Friday night.

Pictures of Kyle at school events with his Ethan, Kate, and Mary adorned every inch of space on his shelves that wasn't already taken over by books. A poster of Kyle in a white karate gi unleashing a spinning high kick hung on the back of his bedroom door.

The alarm on his bedside table read 9:45 AM, and he held back a groan as he hauled himself out of bed. He was late. Again.

He felt groggy from lack of sleep, and blamed the crazy dream he'd had about charging across an enormous field on Terra with his friends, charging into a battle with wolves and tigers by his side. Maybe he should consider cutting back on their game time.

He took a few minutes to stretch then practiced a few Karate moves to get the blood flowing and help kick-start his brain. It was still foggy from remnants of the weird dream.

He grabbed some clothes from his closet, not particularly caring what they were since no one would see what he was wearing from his chest down when they connected on the computer. He picked up his cell phone, thumbed through his email to check for anything important, then snagged his laptop and headed for the kitchen.

The day was over-cast, but that didn't matter much to Kyle. Over-cast meant less distractions and he could spend more time with Ethan in the garage tinkering with their current project. He made himself some cereal, then sat at the breakfast bar to eat while he connected his laptop with the school's online meeting site.

Kyle, as usual, was late getting connected and Mr. Aaron was already on with Ethan, Mary and Kate.

"Can't wait to see your project." Mr. Aaron was already chatting with the group, but noticed when Kyle came into the chat room. "Glad you could join us, Kyle. You're late again."

"Sorry, Mr. Aaron, I over-slept." Kyle knew it was a lame excuse, but it happened to be true this time.

"I expect better from you. The competition is tight and I'm counting on you to pull a rabbit out of your hat." Mr.

Aaron paused to let that sink in. "I'm putting you in charge of the group, Kyle, so no more tardiness. How does that make you feel?"

"Fine, I guess." Actually, Kyle felt anything but fine about being appointed the leader of the group. Any one of his friends would do a better job, and he looked hopefully at the others in their square boxes on the screen hoping one of them would speak up and tell Mr. Aaron what a dumb idea it was.

Kyle checked the Chat section at the bottom of the screen in case Mary had something to say to the group. Even though she hadn't spoken since she was a kid, she could still hear perfectly, and would type her responses to them. But even she had no argument.

"Great, then let's wrap up for now. Everyone remember to have fun. You're going to be great. I'll see you all Friday." Mr. Aaron loved a good pep-talk. "Kyle can you hang on for a minute?"

"Sure Mr. Aaron." Kyle figured he was about to get yelled at for his chronic tardiness, but at least he was at home and not surrounded by all the other kids in his class.

Ethan and Kate said their good-byes and closed out of the session. Mary waved enthusiastically before she, too, left the session.

"Your team needs you to lead by example, Kyle." Mr. Aaron didn't pull any punches, and got right to the point. "You're a good student, but you're not up to snuff lately. Is everything okay with you? Is there anything you want to talk about?"

Kyle's back tensed, but he tried to put on a positive face. He didn't want to talk to his teacher about his weird dream, especially with it being so fresh.

"Yeah, sure." He shrugged, and hoped Mr. Aaron would let it go.

"You know this is just between us, so what's on your mind?" Obviously, Mr. Aaron wasn't letting it go.

Kyle knew he was only trying to be helpful, and relaxed slightly. Maybe Mr. Aaron would be a good person to talk to about the dream.

"I had a strange dream last night. I've never had anything like it before." Kyle scrutinized the man on the screen in front of him, checking to see if he would laugh at him. But Mr. Aaron only looked concerned.

"What kind of dream?"

"I'm not sure..." It was hard to put into words, and not simply because it was a dream. "Weird stuff about a war, magical weapons, and a crazy King." Hearing it out loud made it sound even more ridiculous than in his head. "Sounds crazy, right?"

"I'll admit it's different." Mr. Aaron smiled, but it was a kind and supportive smile that made Kyle feel understood. "But I don't think it's crazy. Sometimes dreams can be your subconscious trying to tell you something. And then again it could just be a product of an over active imagination." Mr.

Aaron chuckled, and Kyle felt a weight lift.

"Or too much video time." Kyle rolled his eyes letting Mr. Aaron know that he wasn't taking everything too seriously.

"That too." Mr. Aaron was always telling his students to get outside more. "But I don't think it's anything to worry about."

"Yeah, you're right. Thanks, Mr. Aaron." Kyle's cell phone rang, and the screen indicated that it was Ethan calling.

"Okay, Kyle, I'll let you go." Mr. Aaron must have heard Kyle's phone ring. "See you on Friday."

"Thanks Mr. Aaron." Kyle closed his computer and connected with Ethan on his cell. "Hey, what's up?"

"How fast can you get over here? This thing is gonna blow your mind!" Ethan's volume made Kyle believe Ethan was the one who was about to blow.

"So it's finished?" Kyle was excited now, too. "Yeah, I did it." Ethan was definitely the brains in their group, so it wasn't surprising that he'd been able to push through to find the solution.

"Is the gang there yet?" Kyle didn't want to be the last one there, especially since he'd just agreed -- sort of -- to Mr. Aaron's request that he take on a leadership role.

"They're on the way." Ethan sounded like he could barely contain the excited energy inside. "How soon can you get here?"

"About 15, 20 minutes." Kyle ran up to his room to find his shoes and get himself ready.

"Hurry!" Yep, Ethan was about to go nuclear, and Kyle couldn't help but laugh.

He disconnected the call and glanced outside while he finished getting dressed. Rain splashed against the window, and he figured he was going to need something more water-proof than his hoodie.

# CHAPTER THREE

By the time Kyle reached Ethan's garage, he was soaked to the skin. One more year before he could get his license and not have to ride his bike everywhere. Mary and Kate had beaten him there, and were inside the garage with Ethan.

Kyle was always astonished by how Ethan could do anything in this garage. It was filled with old crumbling storage boxes containing all kinds of electronic parts that Ethan frequently re-purposed for whatever project he was working on at any given moment. There was an old lawn mower that Ethan fixed for his dad on a regular basis.

Fluorescent strip lights were mounted in the ceiling and two ultraviolet lights hung suspended over Ethan's work table. The table itself was covered in electrical equipment, wires and tubes, and so many odd contraptions Ethan had cobbled together over the past few years.

In the middle of all the chaos was Ethan's latest invention. It was twice the size it had been the last time Kyle had seen it.

He had been right about thinking Ethan was on an energetic high. Ethan was bouncing in place while he typed on an old TRS 80 Radio Shack computer connected to an analog TV. The whole thing was connected to a large futuristic-looking computer with colorful lights and glowing buttons.

In a safe spot away from all the machinery and gadgets, Ethan's pet hamster, Elwood, jogged on his wheel inside his cage. Kyle thought

Elwood must know something was up, too, because he was racing faster than usual.

Kate and Mary were watching in fascination, and none of them even noticed when Kyle joined them.

"This is it guys." Ethan faced all three of them, but his eyes sparked so brightly that Kyle wasn't sure he was even seeing any of them. This was Ethan "In the zone," and Kyle knew crazy, exciting things were about to happen.

"What's 'it'?" Kyle stared at the computer, but couldn't figure out what phase of the project Ethan was supposed to be in at this point.

"I give up," Kate said, sounding almost bored. "It's a toaster." Mary's hands signed the words so quickly Kyle almost missed them.

Apparently, Ethan was going to have to come up with something pretty amazing to get everyone up to his level of excitement.

"This transporter can move matter from one point in time to another." Ethan looked expectantly at the group, but Kyle couldn't understand what all the drama was about.

"Mom can do that with her van." Apparently, Kate was in the same what's-the-big-deal boat as Kyle.

"I'm going to ignore you now," replied Ethan, sounding offended.

"You know I'm just messin' with you little brother." Kate punched Ethan lightly in the shoulder, then threw her arm around his neck. She gave him a quick kiss on his head, and Ethan tried to brush off both the kiss and his sister.

"What I'm trying to tell you all is that this is a time machine." Ethan looked smug, as if waiting for a round of applause or something.

"Uh, huh, right." Kate wasn't buying any of it. "That's impossible."

But Kyle wasn't sure what he believed. "You're serious?" Ethan was wicked smart, so Kyle wasn't ready to dismiss him as quickly as Kate. But a time machine? Was that even possible outside of the movies?

Mary, ever the peace-keeper of their group appeared to be willing to suspend her disbelief because she signed, "How does it work?"

Ethan placed an apple on an 'X' he'd taped on a folding table under the futuristic-looking computer.

"This is my second machine," Ethan explained as he started typing on the keyboard. "The first one caught fire."

"That sounds reassuring." Kyle surreptitiously searched the garage for a fire extinguisher just in case.

Thunder cracked and lightning flashed outside as the rain continued to pour. Kyle felt like he was in the middle of one of those movies with the crazy doctor trying to bring a dead body back to life.

Ethan closed the garage door then went back to typing on the old Radio Shack computer. Kyle watched in fascination as words appeared on the TV screen.

'SYSTEM SYNCING. PLEASE WAIT'

Everyone waited until a moment later when more words appeared.

'SYSTEM READY' 'ENTER RUN TIME'

Kyle continued to stare watching the cursor on the screen blink in anticipation of the next command. Ethan typed in the numbers 00:03:00.

"Here we go." Ethan's voice was a whisper, as if he, too, wasn't sure what was going to happen next. He grabbed the TV remote and pointed it at the screen.

"A TV remote?" Kate sounded incredulous and looked like she was going to start laughing.

"It's the perfect trigger device." Ethan glared at his sister until she got herself back under control, then pressed the "ENTER" button on the remote.

The machine flared to life and the screen displayed the words:

'TRANSMISSION IN PROGRESS 00:03:00

The apple on the table glowed as beams of light swirled around it before it vanished entirely.

The screen displayed the words: 'TRANSMISSION COMPLETE'

'END PROCESS'

A digital clock appeared on the screen counting down the time:

'00:02:59'

'00:02:58'

'00:02:57'

Ethan took a step back from the computer and smiled at the group.

"Holy freakin' crap!" Kyle didn't know about the others, but he was as blown away as Ethan had predicted he would be.

"Wow!" Mary signed the word with such deliberateness that Kyle could tell she was feeling the same way.

"So where did it go?" Kate, ever practical, asked the question Kyle knew they were all thinking.

"It didn't go anywhere," Ethan replied, shrugging his shoulders as if her question wasn't significant. "Technically it's still here."

Kate reached into the empty space where the apple had been and waggled her hand around. "Then why can't we see it?"

"Because it's matter." Ethan shrugged his shoulders once more, and Kyle was beginning to wish he'd paid more attention in Science class. "Matter can be converted into energy. I sent it into the future where it reassembled itself back into matter. In essence I poked a hole through space and time and the apple traveled three minutes into the future."

All three of them stared at Ethan like he was speaking a foreign language.

"I'm impressed." Kyle finally broke the silence. He had always known Ethan was smart, but this was pure genius. How had he figured all of this out?

"Are you for real?" Kate was looking at her younger brother as if she had never met him before.

"You saw it yourself," said Ethan, then pointed at the empty spot on the table as if that explained everything. "We'll see the apple again when we catch up to it in its time."

"I'm confused," Mary signed, and Kyle nodded his head in agreement. He looked at the screen, which now read '00:02:00'

"Hang on..." Ethan dug into his pocket and pulled out some loose change of dimes, nickels and quarters. He set them down on the table grouping three quarters and one nickel together.

"Let's say these coins are us," he said, pointing at the quarters.

"Hang on," interrupted Kate. "Who's the nickel in this scenario?"

"Doesn't matter," Ethan replied, quickly getting back to the subject. "This dime is the apple." Ethan picked up the dime and showed it to them like he was performing a magic trick.

"At this moment we're all in the now_time." Ethan placed

the dime several inches to the left of the other group of coins. "Now, the apple," he continued, pointing to the dime, "is in the future."

Ethan slowly moved the group of coins closer to the dime. "With every passing second this is us moving closer in our time to where the apple is in its time."

"In a few seconds, we'll have caught up to the apple's time." He moved the group of coins closer until they joined the dime.

"I get it now. I think," Mary signed, her hands fluttering in excitement.

The computer beeped a signal that caught everyone's attention and drew them back to the screen, which read:

'SYNCING'

The apple appeared back on the "X" in exactly the same spot as if it had never disappeared, and the computer screen read:

'END PROCESS.'

# CHAPTER FOUR

"Holy crap!" Kyle almost couldn't believe his own eyes. If he hadn't seen the looks of astonishment on his friends's faces, he might not have believed it had happened at all. The whole concept was too crazy to comprehend.

"From the apple's point of view," said Ethan, as he continued explaining, "we were here all the time. It's just we were in its past like a TV rerun. It can see us, but it can't interact with us until our time synced. We couldn't see it because it wasn't here until the three minutes had passed."

"Wow, like magic." Kate looked as impressed as Kyle had ever seen her. She, like her brother, had a very scientific mind, and Kyle knew that if she couldn't prove something, it didn't exist. So, for her, calling this magic was a really big deal.

Ethan beamed, apparently thinking the same thing Kyle was about Kate's reaction. "Science does feel like magic sometimes."

Lightening flashed outside the garage door windows, and Kyle counted two Mississippis before the crack of thunder followed. The storm was getting closer, which meant he wasn't going to be biking home anytime soon.

Mary clapped her hands to get everyone's attention before she signed, "Can it do people too?"

"Let's find out." Ethan glanced at ELWOOD who was happily munching in his cage. The poor little guy was completely oblivious to the goings-on of the four humans, and Kyle felt nervous for him.

"No way," Mary signed with deliberate emphasis. She must have felt the same as Kyle about using something alive as a guinea pig for Ethan's experiments. Even if he was a technically a hamster.

"You're gonna use Elwood?" Kate seemed equally as appalled.

Ethan retrieved Elwood from his cage and placed him on the 'X' in a glass container. Elwood didn't seem concerned, which Kyle took as a reassuring sign.

Mary wasn't convinced. "Are you sure he'll be okay?" she signed.

"I wouldn't try it if it wasn't safe." Ethan seemed sure of the experiment, which convinced Kyle that it would be safe.

They all watched closely as Ethan adjusted the time on the computer for one minute.

The digital timer on the screen read:

'00:01:00'

A second later the screen displayed the word 'READY'.

Ethan pressed the "ENTER" button on the TV remote, and the screen displayed the words, 'TRANSMISSION IN PROGRESS'.

Elwood began to glow. For a second, he froze then he vanished.

The screen displayed the words 'END PROCESS' and the timer began counting down the seconds as they all watched.

"Now we wait." Ethan sounded a bit like that mad scientist in the movies, but Kyle decided not to point that out to everyone.

Thunder clapped loudly outside causing the whole group to jump.

"Anyone want a soda?" Ethan looked calm on the outside, but Kyle knew he was just as worried about his pet as the rest of them were. Then again, Ethan didn't usually conduct experiments on Elwood that might be considered dangerous, so Elwood was probably going to be fine.

Ethan handed out sodas from the cooler he kept in the garage. Kyle knew from previous experience that Ethan could sometimes forget to eat or drink anything when he was "in the zone" on one of his projects.

Once, Kyle had found Ethan swaying on his feet and speaking gibberish. It freaked Kyle out so much that he brought the cooler into the garage and kept it stocked with sodas and vitamin waters to keep Ethan fueled. Kyle lived in fear that he would stop by one day and find Ethan passed out on the ground.

The computer beeped its signal and everyone turned automatically to watch the 'X'.

The screen displayed the word 'SYNCING' and the hamster appeared exactly on the 'X' where it left looking as if nothing strange had happened.

The screen displayed the words, 'END PROCESS' and everyone cheered.

"Cooool," Mary signed.

Ethan checked Elwood over and put him back in his cage. "It works." Kyle was stunned. Ethan had actually completed their project. It was no longer theoretical for them. They had discovered time travel. This was huge. "You're a genus!"

They spent the next several minutes congratulating and high-fiving each other, and Kyle was feeling really proud of their small team. This was an incredible thing they had put together. Ethan was obviously the brain behind the whole thing, but they had all contributed to the calculations and mechanics of the project.

"So who wants to be the first to go?" Ethan spoke the words, and everyone went so quiet that Kyle could hear Elwood munching in his cage. Outside, the wind splattered raindrops on the garage door windows.

"Go where?" Mary signed.

Ethan smiled at her -- the answer to her question obvious.

"Oh, no," Kate said, then snorted. "I'm not going in that thing."

But Kyle was excited. Why not see where it would take them? It was only three minutes. "Come on, Kate. We're in this together. Remember? And it'll be fun. Aren't you the least bit curious?"

"You know you wanna," Ethan said, encouraging Kate. "We stick together. Come on, it'll be a blast."

"I think it's crazy," Mary signed to Kate, "but they're right. We're together. I'm in."

They all gave their most pleading looks at Kate, who Kyle could tell was beginning to weaken.

"OK." Kate finally caved to the pressure. "But if anything happens I will haunt you all forever."

"Yes!" Ethan did a fist pump. "This is going to be awesome."

Kyle didn't feel nearly as confident at Ethan, but figured they were all in this together.

What could possibly go wrong?

# CHAPTER FIVE

Kyle decided it was best to stay out of Ethan's way while he did whatever preparations were needed to shoot all of them through time. He moved over to the garage windows and watched the rain pouring down outside. Lightening flashed and he only got in one Mississippi before the clap of thunder that followed.

The storm was worse than before, and he knew he would either have to call his mom for a ride home, or stay the night with Ethan. Ethan's mom and dad were like his second parents. They never minded when Kyle showed up unexpectedly and stayed the night. They were cool about that kind of thing.

Kyle's mom always needed more advanced warning. Why? Kyle had no idea. It wasn't like two fifteen-year-old boys really cared how the house looked, or even what she was serving for dinner. But whatever.

"I've widened the beam so we'll all transport together." Ethan's voice cut into Kyle's thoughts, and reminded him they were on the verge of something really big. "Everyone put on these wrist devices."

Ethan handed each of them a device that looked suspiciously like watches to Kyle. But what did he know about Ethan's inventions?

Mary examined the device and signed the very question that had been on Kyle's mind. "What are these watches for?"

"They're not watches." Ethan gave Mary a very condescending look, and Kyle was glad he hadn't been the one to ask the question. "I call them

'Wrist Comms.' They allow the time machine to track us wherever we go in time and bring us back here."

"All in one piece I hope." Kate still didn't seem convinced this was a good idea, and Kyle didn't blame her. He trusted Ethan, but this was a whole new level of trust. Still, he was glad she was coming with them.

Even though Kyle was technically dating Lynn, he'd always had a major crush of Ethan's older sister. Lynn was never interested in the stuff Kyle did with his friends. She didn't even try to understand the math and science that he, Ethan, Mary and Kate thrived on.

"Notice the screens on the watches." Ethan apparently decided to ignore Kate's skepticism, and got on with his instructions.

Kyle looked at his watch, then glanced at everyone else's, noticing they were all green.

"The green means the device has a good lock on us." "I'm scared." Mary signed.

"Me too." Kate whispered the words, and Kyle felt a shiver run down his spine. Should they stop?

"As long as the comms are green the machine can pull us back to our time no matter where we are." Ethan sounded so confident, it helped make Kyle feel better. "No problem at all."

Ethan made more adjustments to the computer while Kyle watched Mary and Kate. They both watched Ethan with what looked like part excitement and part dread.

"This is the longest time I've tried." Ethan sounded like he was talking to himself, as if he'd forgotten the rest of them were there.

"Hang on, you never mentioned that." Kyle wasn't sure if that was a good thing or a bad thing.

"Here we go." Ethan either hadn't heard Kyle, or he did care. He pressed the "ENTER" button on the TV remote, and the decision was done.

Kyle watched the computer screen as the words 'TRANSMISSION IN PROGRESS' appeared. At the same time, he saw a flash of lightening and the power in the garage went out.

Then everything went dark.

# CHAPTER SIX

He could hear sounds, but he couldn't see anything. For a moment Kyle hit maximum panic overload. Then he realized his eyes were still shut, and he opened them gently.

It was still overcast, but at least the rain had stopped pouring. The wind picked up, and he heard thunder in the distance. He didn't even bother counting Mississippis because it was too far away to be a danger to them.

Kyle sat up and looked around. How did they end up in a forest? Ethan's house wasn't anywhere near trees like these. These trees were huge and there were so many of them.

The garage was gone, too. His friends were beginning to wake up from whatever they had just gone through, too.

"What a ride!" Ethan was thrilled, and Kyle suspected he hadn't started to look around yet.

"Holy crap." Kate sat up holding her head. Kyle could relate. He'd never had a hangover before, but thought it must be the same as what he was feeling. His head felt like it was going to fall off. Considering how much it was pounding, he didn't think he'd care if it did fall off.

"What happened to the garage?" Mary signed to the group, then looked around in confusion.

"Where are we?" Kyle wasn't asking that question to anyone specifically. He was pretty sure they were all as confused as he was, but he needed to ask it anyway.

"Are you kidding me?" Kate didn't sound happy, and she was facing in the opposite direction of everyone else.

Kyle was afraid to turn around, but he did it anyway.

They were on an island, surrounded by water as far as he could see.

"Holy crap." Ethan didn't sound nearly as excited as he'd been when they first woke up.

"What happened, Ethan?" Kyle was beginning to panic. This wasn't three minutes into the future in Ethan's garage. They were...

Well, that was the problem, he had no idea where they were.

"I don't know." Ethan sounded more confused than concerned, which helped calm Kyle down. But not by much.

Especially when jagged bolts of lightning cracked the sky overhead.

"Now what?" Mary signed her question.

"We have to get out of here, Ethan." Kate's voice cracked, and Kyle could see the panic in her face. "Quick send us back."

"Hurry," Mary signed. "I'm getting soaked." She was right, it had started to rain again.

"I don't have a lock." Ethan began tapping his wrist comm and moving it around like he was checking for a cell signal or something.

Kyle looked at his comm, and it was completely dark.

Hadn't Ethan told them that their comms would be green when the system had a lock on them? Lightning sparked the sky followed immediately by a big "Boom!"

"We have to get out of this weather and find shelter.

It's not safe out here." Kyle wasn't usually afraid of storms, but he also knew it wasn't a good idea to be in the middle of one when there was lightning.

"Look!" Kate pointed to a small path that Kyle hadn't seen yet. "It looks like it leads to an old looking beach house."

"Where did that come from?" So, Ethan hadn't seen the path before either.

"It wasn't there a second ago." Kate shrugged, as if it didn't matter, but she still looked worried.

How was that even possible? Paths didn't just magically show up when you needed them. But Kyle was not going to ignore this one. "It's there now, so let's go."

"Are you sure it's a good idea?" Mary was signing so quickly, Kyle almost could keep up with her. "What if someone's in there?"

It was an excellent question, but they didn't have many options. "We can't stay out here. We need cover." Kyle looked up at the sky that had darkened even more as they'd talked.

They all took off at a run, and made it to the beach house just as another bolt of lightning hit the sky. They stood huddled together on the front porch, looking at each other for someone to decide what to do next.

Kyle sighed, realizing they would all be standing out there forever if he didn't do something. He knocked on the door, but no one answered. He moved to the front window and peeked inside through one of the cracks between the boards that covered it up.

The house looked like no one had lived there in a very long time. The boarded windows were his first clue, but there were also covers over the furniture. It appeared to be empty so he went back to the front door and reached for the knob.

The door opened by itself.

"Ooooooookaaaay..." Ethan sounded like he was going to laugh, and Kyle didn't appreciate it. Then again, he must have looked pretty stupid standing there with his arm raised and his hand forming a knob-shaped circle with nothing in it.

Kyle dropped his hand and turned to glare at Ethan, but there wasn't any conviction in it.

"Yeah, so, that just happened." Kate's sarcastic voice usually showed up when she didn't know how to handle the situation. She must have been really thrown by this whole thing.

"Come on," Kyle said. It was time to take on the role of leadership. Ethan did all things technical, but he sucked at leading.

Kyle gathered his courage and lead them inside the house.

The door opened for them, which had to be a welcome invitation. Right? How scary could this be?

The house looked gloomy and lonely. The only light came from what filtered in through the cracks and spaces between the boarded up windows. And that light wasn't very bright considering the sky outside.

Kyle debated leaving the door open for the light, or shutting it against the wind, and decided they needed the light, so he left it open.

Ethan flicked a switch on the wall and the light hanging from the ceiling illuminated. It wasn't much, but it was better than the dark. The wind outside howled and whistled through the cracks in the walls giving the house an ethereal feeling.

Kyle wondered if ghosts would start to show up and tell them to leave. Probably not if they'd gone to the trouble of opening the front door to welcome them inside. Besides, he didn't believe in ghosts.

Much.

"Spooky," Ethan said, as if reading Kyle's mind. "This reminds me of those old mystery movies." Kate sounded like she was getting over her nerves.

"There's something written on that wall." Kyle couldn't read them from where he stood, but there were definitely words on the wall at the other side of the room.

"Where?" Kate was right behind him.

"Right there." Kyle moved closer, leaning in to get a better look.

"There's nothing there." Ethan leaned in and examined the wall, but shook his head at Kyle.

Kyle didn't understand why Ethan was being so dense, but the best thing to do when he was acting like a jerk was to ignore him.

"It says," Kyle said, glaring at Ethan, 'You came to this place by chance, but you'll leave it with a mission'."

"What does that mean?" Mary signed to the group, but she seemed to be asking it rhetorically.

"It means," said Ethan with authority in his voice, "someone is messing with us and we're getting out of here."

The front door slammed shut and locked, causing them all to jump and turn around at the same time. Ethan snapped out of it first, and went over to the door. He struggled with the knob and tried to yank the door open but couldn't get it to budge.

"The message is gone." Kyle couldn't believe his eyes.

Where had it gone? They had all seen it. Right?

"I'm very worried now," Mary signed, and Kyle could see that her hands shook slightly.

"We should get out of here." Kate sounded like she was working up a good panic as well.

"Update, Kate: We can't." Ethan tended to turn snarky when he was nervous.

The wind outside picked up, howling, and the lights in the house flickered.

"Who are you?" asked a loud male voice that reverberated through the house.

# CHAPTER SEVEN

"Did anyone else hear that?" Kate asked in a whisper, and Kyle thought she might have hoped they would all say, "No." But he'd heard it, too.

"I heard it," Mary signed.

Then it dawned on Kyle. "Stop fooling around Ethan. You aren't funny."

"It wasn't me." His face went pale, so Kyle knew it couldn't have been Ethan. He wasn't that good at acting.

"Who are you?" The mysterious voice boomed again. "Someone's here?" Mary signed, and Kyle wondered if ghosts could understand sign language.

"We need to search the house and find him," Kate said, her voice barely above a whisper.

"Mary, you go that way," Ethan said, and gestured her toward a hallway on the right. She gave him a nervous nod, but headed in the direction he'd indicated. "I'm going to check the back of the house."

Ethan turned in a circle, apparently unsure about where the back of the house was. He must have made up his mind, because he headed in the opposite direction that Mary had just gone. Kate and Kyle were alone in the main entryway.

"Guess I'll head upstairs." Kate didn't sound like this was something she wanted to do, but marched herself to the stairs anyway. Kyle was left alone in the main entry, unsure about where to go or what to do.

"Who are you?" asked the male voice again.

Kyle spun around the room trying to discover where the voice was coming from. How was it possible that it sounded like it was coming from everywhere? Acoustics. That's how. But that was about as much as Kyle knew on the subject.

"Where are you?" Kyle asked. Everything would be much easier if the voice would just answer them.

The house wasn't very big, so the search had only taken a few minutes. Kate, Mary and Ethan all filed back into the main room with Kyle.

"Nothing." Kate seemed more frustrated than scared. "Do you think it's a spirit?" Ethan asked. He didn't appear to be scared either, but he was curious.

"It must be. No one else is here," signed Mary.

"Who are you?" asked the disembodied voice a third time. "Don't answer it," Ethan said. "What if it's some way to control us."

Kyle considered Ethan's theory. Some people believed that if you give someone your name, you give them a power over you. That probably wasn't the case here though. The voice didn't sound evil, just curious.

"I'm Kyle." He hoped he wouldn't regret telling the voice his name. And turn about was fair play, so he asked, "Who are you?"

"Why are you here?" Either the voice ignored Kyle's question, or he hadn't heard it.

Kyle was pretty sure none of them knew where "here" was, let alone why they were there. "Just sheltering from the storm. We saw the house and came in."

"Where have you come from?"

"We're from Denver." Kyle sure hoped they weren't too far from home.

The room was silent and Kyle looked at his three friends for what to do next. Ethan shrugged, indicating he was just as baffled as Kyle felt. Had the voice left them? Should someone ask questions?

"Where did he go?" Kate was the only one to voice what they were all probably thinking.

"You must be hungry after your long journey." All four friends jumped when the voice spoke again.

Kyle noticed more words appearing on the same wall as before. He read the message out loud. "Go to the kitchen. Eat whatever you like and use anything here."

He searched the faces of his three best friends, wondering what to do. They all stared at the message on the wall until Mary clapped her hands to get their attention.

"Should we trust him?" she signed.

"No," replied Kate. "But do we have a choice?"

Mary and Kyle both shook their heads. Kyle was feeling hungry, and was at least willing to consider eating. Depending on what the food was. If all they had was fish, he was going to pass. Pizza would be nice though.

"I'm not eating anything in this place." Ethan was emphatic, and Kyle was bummed.

All this talking about food had really worked up his appetite. He didn't care anymore what the food was. He would probably still eat it.

Ethan started searching the furniture in the room. He opened all the drawers in each table and slammed them all shut. When he came up empty, he went down the hallway, and Kyle heard him open squeaking doors to search other rooms. He stood there debating with himself while listening to Ethan opening more drawers then slamming them shut.

After several minutes of hearing banging and muttering Ethan finally returned to the group. He laid a hammer and a small screw driver on the table in the middle of the room. Ethan took the hammer back and scrutinized it.

"What are you going to do with that?" Kyle asked, sincerely believing his friend had finally gone off the deep end. "There's no one else here but us."

"And a spirit." Kate pointed out.

"He offered us food." Kyle could not understand why they weren't all racing into the kitchen by now.

"Some crazy person is playing a sick joke." Ethan wasn't letting it go.

"Then where is he?" Kyle was beginning to wonder if his friend was losing it. Then again, his hunger was probably getting the better of his own judgment. Not that he would ever admit that out loud.

"I don't know and I don't care." Ethan hefted his hammer. "I'm getting out of here." He attacked the door lock before anyone even registered what he'd planned to do.

Nothing happened. The knob wasn't even dented. Ethan pounded it again and again until his energy was spent, and he slumped to the floor.

"Okay, look." Kyle tried to sound as soothing as possible. " We're all scared. But if we keep our heads and stay together we'll get through this. Right?" He was pretty sure he was trying to convince himself as much as the others.

"Fine," Ethan said. He sounded exhausted and more frightened than Kyle had ever heard him. "But I'm keeping this anyway." Ethan hugged the hammer.

Kate wandered off in the direction of the kitchen. At least Kyle assumed it was the kitchen. It was the room Ethan searched earlier when he said he was going to the kitchen.

"It's getting dark," Mary signed to Kyle. "Let's sleep here and see how things are in the morning."

"Hey guys." Kate's voice came from the other room. "Look what I found."

# CHAPTER EIGHT

Kyle was worried about what Kate found, but he really hoped it was food. Edible food.

He followed Mary and Ethan into the room where Kate had gone and was relieved to see it truly was the kitchen. The decor looked like something out of one of those old black and white TV shows his mom liked to watch, but it was a kitchen. There was an oven and a fridge, so that made it a kitchen.

The wallpaper was peeling and the paint was chipped. The appliances looked so old, he was sure they no longer worked.

Kate was standing next to a large wooden table that had six mismatched chairs around it. More important, Kyle could see that the table was covered with food. There was an assortment of fruits, cheeses, meats, breads and several pitchers containing various beverages. Kyle was so hungry, he was sure he could eat it all.

No one moved to sit at the table, let alone touch any of the food. In spite of his overwhelming hunger, Kyle could understand their reluctance to dig right in. Was it was safe to eat? Hadn't he read a story once about being tricked by the fairies into eating food and being trapped in their realm forever?

"I don't think he would poison us. Right?" Kate sounded like she was also torn, and Kyle wondered if she'd read the same fairy stories.

He finally decided they were being ridiculous. Looking at all that food had only increased his hunger. "Let's eat, get some rest and figure this out in the morning."

He grabbed some bread and cheese and shoved it all in his mouth. He couldn't remember when anything had tasted this fabulous. If it killed him, he was definitely going to enjoy himself first.

"Mmmmm, durishish." His mouth was so full, he wasn't sure anyone had understood him, but figured they'd catch on eventually.

They must have decided Kyle's taste testing cleared the food, because all three of them attacked the food at the same time. Ethan even relinquished his hammer long enough to make a sandwich, which Kyle felt was progress.

"We should do a thorough search of the house." Kyle didn't want to pull himself away from the food, but they should make sure they were at least safe in the house. "We can take our sandwiches with us." He wasn't willing to risk the food disappearing when they left the room. He had no idea how it had materialized in the first place. What were the odds it would disappear in the same way just as quickly?

"Okay, but let's stick together this time." Mary signed. Kyle couldn't blame her being nervous to be alone. The house already had disembodied voices and mysteriously appearing food. What else were they going to find?

Ethan started rummaging around in the drawers in the kitchen. Kyle assumed he was still hunting for weapons, which wasn't a bad idea.

"Ah, ha!" Ethan shouted, and everyone jumped. "A Swiss army knife. I think I can use this to fix our comms."

When it came to technology and machines, Kyle knew Ethan could fix anything. Including building a time machine. So, Kyle had hope that Ethan would be able to fix their comms and get them home again.

The four of them left the kitchen. Kyle glanced back at the table feeling bummed that the food would most likely be gone the next time they came back into the kitchen. He only hoped the voice would make them breakfast in the morning.

Feeling much better now that he'd been fed, he followed his friends back into the living room. Mary, Ethan and Kate were frozen in the doorway. Kyle was afraid to look, but he peered over Mary's shoulder to see what had them so stunned.

There were four cozy sleeping bags laid neatly on the floor like spokes on a wheel. A fire had been lit in the fireplace Kyle hadn't even noticed was there.

"Well, how about that." Kyle was feeling even better about the possibility of breakfast in the morning.

"Rest for the night." The house's voice spoke and snapped them out of their stunned state. "In the morning you'll go on your quest."

"Did he say_quest?" Mary signed.

"That's what he said." Kate sounded resigned. "We don't even know his name, and already he's telling us what to do."

"My name is Neal," said the voice.

"Well, that answers that question." Kyle felt somewhat better knowing the voice's name. And Neal sounded like a nice enough name.

"You will travel to the Kendo Kingdom," continued Neal, "and help free the people from their stone sleep." Neal seemed to take it for granted that they would do whatever he said.

"We don't have to do this," Kate said, although she didn't sound convinced. "We can just stay right here."

"I agree," said Ethan. "I'd rather stay here until we can go home. By now the machine must be resetting and will soon lock onto us. You'll see."

Kyle liked the idea of waiting at the house until they could go home again. It was safe here. And as long as Neal, or the house, or whatever kept bringing them food, they would be fine.

"You cannot stay." Neal didn't sound angry, but he did sound firm. "This house is here by magic and will soon return to the netherworld. If you stay you will go with it and not return for one hundred years."

"So, do the math." Ethan sounded like he was considering risking it.

"That settles it." Kyle was not up for playing Russian roulette with magic and ending up in the ether. They'd already done that, and ended up here. "We do the mission and then we're outta' here."

"Wait." Kate was apparently not convinced. "How do we know he's telling the truth? How do we know we can trust him? I don't know if I do. Do you?" She turned to Mary for support.

"Kate makes sense." Mary signed.

"He could be lying, but so what." Kyle knew that Kate had a point, and he didn't want to argue with her, but he wanted to get going. The sooner they completed this stupid quest, to this Kendo Kingdom place, the sooner they could focus on getting back home. "We're stuck here either way so we might as well do something while we wait."

"That makes sense, too." Mary signed.

"Okay, but I'm still not crazy about it." Kate was in, which was a good thing, because Kyle knew they were going to need her if they had any hope of succeeding at whatever this quest was going to be. Having Kate on their team was always a good thing.

He also didn't want to risk leaving Kate behind and never seeing her again for a hundred years.

"Great let's get some sleep." Kyle figured they were going to need it. "Tomorrow is going to be a big day."

"Except that I'm not sleepy." Ethan seemed so wired up, he was practically bouncing off the walls.

Kyle took that as a good sign because when Ethan got going, things happened. Then again, that was how they ended up here in this place, wherever -- whenever -- that was.

"Good, then you can take the first watch." Kyle smacked Ethan on the back for emphasis, and almost knocked him over. "We'll take turns every three hours."

Kyle put out his hand, palm down so that everyone could stack hands on his. "We're in this together?"

For a moment, no one else moved, staring at him, and he worried they weren't going to follow his lead. Then, one by one, they each stacked their hand on top of his in a friendship pile.

"Friends together. Friends forever."

They all shouted like the were in a football huddle before breaking out of the circle. Kyle was relieved that they were still a team. They would get through this and get home together.

Ethan pulled out the Swiss army knife that he'd found earlier and examined it. "I think I might be able to get my comm to connect with the time machine."

Kyle couldn't see how he was going to be able to accomplish that with only a Swiss army knife, but if anyone could do it, Ethan could. "Okay, that's a good idea."

Ethan took his comm off and started working on it, and Kyle knew from past experience that he'd lost Ethan's attention completely. Good. The sooner Ethan figured out his comm, the sooner they could get home.

# CHAPTER NINE

Sunlight beamed through the cracks of the boarded up windows, and Kyle took the solitary moment to enjoy the peace and quiet. He took the last shift to watch, appreciating his time alone to think.

In spite of not knowing where they were, or how to get back home, he was glad he was at least stuck here with his three best friends. They would figure it out together, and get back home one way or another.

Kyle watched his friends sleep, giving them a few extra minutes of peace before they had to face the day. He thought about each of them, and how much they meant to him.

Ethan was the brain of the group. He would no doubt figure out the mechanics to get them home. It could be intimidating how much Ethan knew that Kyle didn't. But Ethan could be so much in his head that he forgot that there was an outside world. It sometimes made social situations very awkward for him.

Mary was their spirit, the one who made sure they were all walking their own path and staying true to themselves. She kept them together and made sure each person's side was heard in any argument. Mary was neutral Switzerland, who noticed things the rest of them missed.

Then there was Kate. She was the heart of their group. Kate had been taking care of Ethan so long it was ingrained. As direct and forceful as she was sometimes, especially under pressure, Kyle knew that it was her mamma-bear-protective way of keeping everyone safe.

Kyle's heart connected to Kate's heart. Technically, he was dating Lynn who was nice. She could also be annoying. Lynn was definitely more into dating Kyle, than he was into dating her. The biggest problem for Kyle was that Lynn wasn't Kate. Kyle knew Kate was way out of his league -- and not only because she was two years older -- but he was glad she at least kept him around as a friend in the group.

He wondered where that left him in the group. He knew they looked to him as the one to make the hard decision when they couldn't all agree. But he didn't always have the answers. Especially in this place. What if this quest they were supposed to take got one of them hurt? Or worse, what if it got someone killed?

He retrieved the four backpacks the house had produced for them. They'd materialized during Kyle's shift, and he's stashed them in the closet. He set a backpack near each of his friends, and gently shook them all awake. He noticed that Ethan's wrist comm was back on his wrist and hoped that meant he'd made progress in fixing it.

"I'll see if the door is open." Kyle went to the front door hoping Neal was letting them out this morning.

He was hesitant to turn the knob. At that moment, it was like Schrodinger's Cat, which they'd learned about in class.

On the one side, it was possible that in the night, Ethan had fixed the time problem, and they were back where they belonged.

Or, on the other side, the time they were in was the same as it had been when they fell asleep, and they would need to go on the quest.

Either way, he wouldn't know for sure until he opened the door.

He opened the door.

# CHAPTER TEN

Whatever had happened with Schrodinger's actual cat, Kyle had discovered when he opened the door and peeked outside, that they were all still in this strange place and time.

They were going on a quest.

"We should get our stuff together." Kate began sorting through the backpack Kyle had set near her.

Kyle rolled up his sleeping bag because his mom had ingrained tidiness into the very fiber of his being. Then he went to the kitchen and found four neatly packed boxes of food -- one for each of them. Dang. He was really going to miss this house and its magical food dispenser. He picked up the boxes and returned to the group in the living room.

"Did you get it to work?" Kate was holding Ethan's hand, examining his wrist comm.

"Yes. And, no." Ethan didn't notice the flash of hope which morphed into despair that crossed Kate's face. But Kyle saw it.

"It's working," Ethan continued. "It's just not connected to home. So I guess we'll be here for a while longer."

"The door's unlocked." Kyle tried not to sound as disappointed as he felt, but wasn't sure how well he succeeded. All eyes turned to the door as it swung open on its own.

The air seemed calm, and Kyle felt a slight breeze coming in off the sea. The sand appeared to still be damp from the morning tide, and he wanted nothing more than to stay here with this house and his friends. He'd always loved the water, and secretly dreamed of owning his own boat.

As if his thoughts conjured it, a boat materializes on the beach. It was a large pirate ship with a massive balloon floating at the top.

"What is that?" Ethan sounded as surprised as Kyle felt. "A balloon with a boat attached to it." Kyle was glad he wasn't hallucinating, but he wasn't sure what they were supposed to do next.

Mary seemed giddy with excitement, vibrating with enthusiasm.

Whereas, Kate appeared to be rendered speechless. Her speechless worried Kyle more than the anticipation of the quest. Kate was never at a loss for words.

"Your journey begins with this vessel." Noah's bodyless voice emanated all around them, and Kyle jumped in surprise. "It will take you to the place of the rising waters and your next destination."

"Our ride has arrived." Ethan seemed more excited than Kyle felt he should be, given their situation. But Ethan was always a risk-taker. He ran toward the boat like an eager four year old going on an adventure.

No one else moved, until Kyle decided they didn't have any other choice. "We might as well get aboard," he said, and he hoped he sounded more determined than nervous. He doubted it.

"Be careful." Noah's voice called after them. "King Warren knows you're here and he won't be happy to see you."

Because that didn't sound ominous at all. Kyle kept his sarcasm to himself, because he didn't want to increase the already high level of tension, but he was not a fan of dire warnings.

"Who's King Warren?" he asked Noah.

"He turned the people to stone with his magic sword," Noah replied. "He's very powerful and extremely dangerous."

"Sounds like a fun guy." Kyle regretted saying the words out loud as soon as they were out of his mouth. So much for keeping his sarcasm to himself.

They all made their way to the balloon boat, and climbed the gang plank to land on the deck. It was not like any boat Kyle had ever seen before. There were huge metal fans blowing into a mostly collapsed white, silky balloon in the middle of the deck.

The rest of the boat was constructed out of a deep, dark wood polished to a shine. Kyle ran his hands over it, gliding over its smooth finish. There were sails hanging from the front of the boat made out of the same material as the balloon. Kyle's instincts were telling him that the boat was yearning to be in the air.

Next to the entrance of the deck was a simple control panel with a single button. One word was etched into a silver plate that said, 'PRESS'.

"You're kidding me." Kate finally spoke, and Kyle felt relieved.

"What does that mean?" Mary signed, obviously as confused as the rest of them.

"Press it, and we'll find out." Ethan smiled, as if they were playing a game.

Mary and Kate both turned and looked at Kyle as if he had all the answers. He didn't.

He pressed the button anyway.

A loud grating sound came from the fans as they began to slowly rotate, and the ship felt like it was coming alive. The fans built up in speed and began filling the balloon to its full size. It was massive.

Kyle had never seen a balloon up close like this, and he was awestruck by its size. Wind from the ocean filled the front sails and the vessel ascended into the sky.

The sun was bright, the sky was clear, and the birds were chirping. In spite of the frightening warnings from a ghost, Kyle couldn't help but think that it was a perfect day for a balloon ride.

This quest-thing was going to be a piece of cake.

# CHAPTER ELEVEN

Kyle stared out across the horizon watching as the sun took its time rising in the sky. It was a beautiful sunrise, but he wished he could have taken his time to wake up like this lazy sun. No one had complained that he'd roused them early, so perhaps they were all as anxious to get moving as he'd been.

He studied the horizon, wondering why it looked so different to him. The sky was a beautiful blue, cloudless expanse with three barely visible full moons hovering in the distance. They looked as if they were falling asleep at the same time the sun was waking up. Each one larger than the other.

Wait a second.

Three moons? How was that possible?

"Hey, check it out." Kyle waved his hand to get everyone's attention, beckoning them to join him at the side of the boat.

"Where are we?" Kate sounded more confused than frightened, which Kyle took as a positive thing.

"Cool." Mary signed, dragging out the gesture in emphasis. Her eyes were bugging out of her head, so Kyle caught the expression without her exaggerated hand gesture.

"I don't think we're on earth any more," Ethan said. "At least not ours."

"What do you mean 'not ours'?" Kyle didn't like the sound of that at all.

"Do you remember what happened right after I activated the time machine?" Ethan looked like he was trying to process files in his brain.

"Yeah," Kate said. "Everything glowed and there were sparks all over the place."

"I think lightning must've hit the machine at the exact time we transported." Ethan sounded matter-of-fact, but Kyle knew a lightening strike couldn't be a good thing. "Must have juiced it and caused a rip in time and space."

Kate didn't say anything else, and Kyle was sure she was processing all of what Ethan had just said. He only hoped she'd come up with some brilliant plan like she usually did, and get them home.

"So what do we do now?" Mary signed.

"Well," Ethan checked his wrist comm. "We can't go home yet. So, let's ride this thing and see what happens."

Kyle checked his wrist comm, then noticed that Mary and Kate both did the same thing. Apparently, he wasn't the only one who wasn't as revved up to "see what happens" as Ethan was.

Kyle's comm was dead, so he could only assume theirs were, too. "Looks like we don't have much choice."

"I'm pretending not to be worried." Mary signed. "Yeah me too." Kate put her arm around Mary in camaraderie and probably even commiseration. Kyle could definitely relate.

"I'm going to explore the ship." Ethan took off and opened the first door he found.

Kyle figured there was nothing else to do, since the boat seemed to be flying itself. He only hoped it knew where it was going. He followed Ethan through the door.

Apparently, Mary and Kate had the same train of thought, because they followed as well.

The room was the same dark wood as the rest of the ship, the entire back wall lined in cabinets. Ethan began a thorough search, although Kyle wasn't sure what Ethan hoped to find.

Inside the first cabinet he opened, Ethan pulled out a dusty burlap sack. It had a draw string and looked like one of those old gunnysacks Kyle's mom always brought home from her favorite natural shop. He half expected them to find a bunch of coffee beans inside or something.

Ethan opened the sack, which Kyle thought was either really brave or really stupid. Who knew what could be inside that bag? It looked like it had been there a million years.

Ethan dug inside, and pulled out a large crystal ball.

That was probably the last thing Kyle had been expecting. But considering the things his mom bought in her natural shop, it wasn't entirely a surprise. As Ethan studied the ball, it began to glow and vibrate, the light inside crackling and shifting.

"I've never seen anything like this before." Ethan rotated the ball in several directions examining it with a look of awe. "The way that stuff inside moves."

They all stood mesmerized and watched as light blossomed inside the ball. Ethan went into some kind of trance, and the room filled with a giant 3-D hologram. It showed a beautiful palace adorned with silver and gold, and a statue of the god Poseidon guarded the entrance of a large stone city.

"This is Atlantis." Ethan continued to stare at the ball but he began speaking in a hollow voice Kyle had never heard him use before. "The citizens were happy. Their technology was so advanced, it was like magic to us."

"A volcano erupted," Ethan continued. Kyle and the others watched as fire and smoke exploded around the city. "Fire fell from the sky. And before the people realized, lava had consumed the city." The image in the ball zoomed in on a small area. "This island is all that remains of Atlantis."

Ethan blinked several times as the images faded and the crystal ball returned to normal.

# CHAPTER TWELVE

"Why is everyone staring at me?" Ethan appeared genuinely confused, and Kyle could only assume he'd completely blanked through the trance.

"The ball glowed," Kyle said by way of explanation. "Then you went into a trance and started rambling about Atlantis."

"The whole room turned into a holographic movie." Kate sounded like she was equal parts impressed and freaked out. Kyle knew that she was trying to cover up the freaked out part.

"Atlantis?" Mary signed. "Awesome." She smiled, but she didn't look completely convinced.

"I thought it was just a myth." Kyle remembered hearing about it somewhere. Science? Biology? English Lit?

"I remember now." Ethan scrunched up his face as if trying to piece it all together. "It was like I was there." "Can you get it to tell us how to get home?" Kyle wasn't sure he trusted the thing, but it was worth a shot.

"I don't know," Ethan replied. "It seems to kind of tell me things on its own. I think we're mind linked or something."

Ethan held the ball in the front of him and closed his eyes as if trying to focus.

"Nothing's happening." Kyle didn't expect it to work, but he was still disappointed.

"Lemme try again." Again, Ethan closed his eyes, then scrunched up his face. "It's not working and I think I'm getting a headache."

"We'll figure it out." To hide his disappointment, Kyle smiled and gave Ethan a bro-slap on the back.

Ethan returned the crystal ball to the sack and set it aside to continue rummaging around in the cabinets. Apparently pleased with the success of Ethan's find, the others began searching the cabinets as well.

"Look! A treasure chest." Ethan proudly held an old small gold box with an inscription on the top.

They all stopped their own search to watch Ethan open the box. He was so excited, Kyle could see his hands shaking with anticipation. Inside the box was a weirdly shaped black pencil with instructions written on an ancient piece of brown material.

The inscription said: <u>You are now the proud owner of the golden box. Use the magic pencil to write a command in the air and it will be so.</u>

"Yeah, right." Kate snorted, ever the skeptic, and Kyle almost laughed.

Ethan shrugged as if he didn't believe it either, then stuffed the pencil in his pocket like he did with all of his other number twos.

Mary pounded on a cabinet door to get everyone's attention, then proudly displayed a small leather pouch that she must have found in one of the other cabinets. She reached inside the pouch and retrieved a dark velvet neck choker.

"It's beautiful and it's probably good luck." Kate was as excited as Mary. "Try it on."

Mary handed the pouch to Kate in order to use both hands, and fastened the choker around her neck. She ran around the deck until she found a mirror to check herself out.

"There's writing on the pouch." Kate had been examining the pouch. "It says, 'Talk to animals'."

"Talk to animals?" Kyle looked over Kate's shoulder to see the inscription himself. "Like Dr. Doolittle?"

"Your guess is as good as mine," Kate said, then shrugged.

"Interesting." Mary signed, then retrieved the pouch from Kate.

Kyle couldn't help but be angry on Mary's behalf. How unfair that she would find a choker to talk to animals when she couldn't speak herself. How would she be able to talk to animals unless they also knew sign language?

He resumed his search of the cabinets. He was trying for nonchalance, but he was seriously excited about finding something for himself. When he found a small sack, similar to the one Ethan had found only smaller, his hopes soared. He opened it, and pulled out a very plain ring.

No markings. No inscriptions. Just a simple silver ring. "Huh." Ethan checked out the ring, obviously unimpressed.

Especially after finding a crystal ball. "Not very interesting to look at. I wonder what it can do?"

It was then that Kyle noticed the writing on the sack. "It says," Kyle read aloud. "'Elemental ring, call them and they will come. Command them and they will do.'"

"Elemental?" Kate joined Kyle, and examined the ring. She had to lean in close enough to touch him, and he almost jumped out of his own skin. He could smell the scent of strawberries that always seemed to follow her around. Strawberries were his favorite fruit.

"I think it's talking about the four seasons," Kate said, but Kyle could barely comprehend. "It means you can call for snow, rain, wind and air."

She stepped back and smiled at him, and he almost fell over. It wasn't as if they'd never been that close before, but Lynn had always been around and Kyle was really careful not to show any feelings for Kate around Lynn.

"Try it," said Ethan, breaking into Kyle's thoughts. "Let's see what happens." Ethan was always good for "seeing what happens." Wasn't that how they'd landed here in the first place?

"Okay..." Kyle wasn't skeptical, but decided to give it a try. "How about...snow?" They all look around, but nothing changes. He'd spoken with a question, and he wondered if he should have spoken with more command. Would that matter?

"Maybe it's nothing." Mary signed. "Only a ring?" "Except that it's getting cold in here." Kate rubbed her arms to warm herself, and Kyle felt goose-bumps along his own arms. A wind picked up and the door to the room blew closed.

They all shivered and began blowing on their hands, shuffling to stay warm. The wind off the ocean howled, and then the sky darkened and it started to snow.

"It works." Kyle was thrilled. Cold, but thrilled. His plain old ring had the ability to make it snow on command. He spun in circles, watching as the snow landed on his outstretched hands.

"Okay, Kyle," Kate said, and her teeth started to chatter. "Fff-feezing over here. Ttt-turn it off now."

"I don't know how." Kyle started to panic. Kate's lips were starting to turn blue and Kyle was afraid she was going to die from exposure. He searched the ring pouch, desperately hoping something would tell him how to turn it off.

"It looks warmer outside." Ethan squinted to look out the window in the door that lead back to the main area of the ship. All four of them bounded to the doorway banging into each other. Kate broke free first, and grabbed the door handle.

"The door's frozen." She rattled the handle several times, but couldn't open the door. "You gotta' do something Kyle."

"Try saying 'Stop snowing?'" Mary signed her suggestion.

Kyle thought he'd already done that, but tried again using different words. "Um - - stop snowing?" Again, it came out like a question, and he wasn't sure if that mattered.

The snow kept falling, so it probably wasn't a good idea to ask as a question. "Stop snowing, please." His mom had taught him to always be polite.

But even being polite didn't stop the snow. And the temperature had gone even colder.

# CHAPTER THIRTEEN

"Wait," Kate said. "I think I've figured it out. Heat is one of the seasons. Right? Try Summer sun before we freeze to death."

"Make it sunny, like Summer." Kyle was getting desperate, and was willing to try anything. And since this was a suggestion from Kate, chances were good it would work.

It stopped snowing.

The dark clouds cleared and the air started to warm up immediately. The heat melted the snow and steam filled the room.

Had the ring really done all that? Or was this ship somehow possessed and magical like the house they'd just left?

"Note to self," Kyle said. "Be careful using this thing." He couldn't decide whether to wear the ring, or put it back in the pouch.

It was easier to wear than to carry, so he slipped it onto his right hand, middle finger. It fit perfectly.

Like it had been made for him.

The main area of the ship was much warmer than the room they'd left, and Kyle was glad to be out in the open air again. He was also glad that Kate was standing next to him at the boat's rail. He still couldn't believe how close he'd come to killing her -- killing all of them -- in that freak snow fall he'd created.

Kate seemed to sense his mood, because she moved closer and bumped him with her shoulder. He glanced up to see her smiling at him, and he knew she didn't hold him responsible. How were any of them to know what would happen in this strange time and place?

He returned her smile, feeling self-conscious, so he leaned over the edge and watched the reflection of the ship in the glistening water below them. They were following the river, but they weren't sailing on it. They were still airborn, but close enough to the water that he could have reached out and run his hand through it.

"It's turning into a real trip." Mary signed, after joining them at the rail.

"I'm bored." Ethan announced from behind them. "I wish something would happen already."

"Be careful what you wish for." Mary signed, then rolled her eyes at Ethan.

"He's never been a fan of road trips." Kate explained, as if Kyle hadn't already witnessed that himself on their last field trip for school. He'd been so bored after twenty minutes in the bus that he'd started doing math problems on the back of one of the seats. The teacher didn't know whether to be impressed or angry.

Ethan was brilliant, but he was also incredibly impatient.

As the balloon traveled along the river, Kyle stood comfortably next to Kate at the bow, wondering if they would be able to continue being this close with each other when they returned to their own time.

He sneaked a glance in her direction and was flustered when she smiled at him. He sifted through his mind for something to say to her, leafing through possibilities as if sorting through clothes on a rack.

"That's different." Kate broke the silence first.

At first Kyle thought she had been speaking to him, and wondered if she had felt the shift of their relationship as he had. But Kate pointed out into the distance, and he followed her line of sight to a waterfall sparkling at the end of the river.

"Weird." Mary signed, as she saw where Kate had pointed. "The water's going up." Kate was the first to figure out why the waterfall had seemed strange.

"You don't see that everyday." Ethan leaned over the rail as if to get a closer look.

"Is that what Spirit Neal was talking about?" Ethan joined them, apparently deciding they finally had something to do.

"That must be the place of the rising waters." Kyle wasn't sure how rising waters equated to a water fall, but things in this world were certainly different than their own.

"So, what's next?" Ethan seemed to be still in his bored phase and couldn't wait for the next thing to do.

"I think we're gonna' find out." Kyle didn't exactly consider himself a planner, but he was better able to handle boredom than Ethan.

The boat continued forward, and Kyle felt a sense of panic as he realized no one was actually piloting -- flying? -- the boat.

"We're headed right for it." Kyle searched for a brake, or a wheel, anything to slow the boat down. They were going to crash. "Hold on!"

The boat came close enough to the backward flowing waterfall they could feel the mist. The boat began to rise along with the ascending waterfall. Kyle was so relieved, he laughed out loud.

"This is crazy!" Mary signed, but Kyle could tell she was as thrilled as he was.

"Yeah it is." Kate joined in the laughter.

The boat continued to rise reaching the clouds and heading beyond the atmosphere.

"Quick everyone," Kyle said, snapping everyone out of their excitement. Things were going to get rough very soon if they kept going up. "Get inside." He turned from the railing and hustled everyone into the closest compartment.

Kyle secured the door on their compartment then joined the others at the windows. They watched the boat climb higher, heading to the stars and the curve of the planet. Misty translucent green auroras formed above them and Kyle gave up on his last thread of hope that they were still on Earth.

# CHAPTER FOURTEEN

"I'm scared," Mary signed to Kate.

"It's okay, we're all scared." Kate held Mary's hand.

Kyle hadn't hit scared yet, but he would have been willing to fake it if Kate would hold his hand, too.

"Not me." Ethan started bouncing around like he'd been shot through with pure adrenaline. "This is so crazy."

The balloon boat drifted close to one of the moons and Kyle started to worry that was going to be their destination. Would they be able to breathe on those moons?

"That must be Terra." Kate's voice was quiet, full of wonder.

The auroras changed to hues of red and the once calm river instantly became a raging torrent.

"What's going on?" Mary signed the question at the same time Kyle thought it in his own head.

"The usual." Ethan sounded nonplussed, but Kyle knew better. He could tell Ethan wasn't as calm has he was trying to portray. "We land in another world. We talk to a ghost that feeds us. A river flows up into the sky, and we're riding in a boat with a balloon on top. Happens all the time."

The raging river churned, getting angrier by the minute, and Kyle felt the boat shifting to descending.

"We're going down hold on." He felt like he was repeating himself, but didn't know what else to say. They weren't dropping quickly, but enough that he was worried they would all get tossed around if they weren't careful.

The boat landed hard on the choppy waters. For several minutes, the boat churned with the water and Kyle didn't know what to do next.

"What's happening?" Kate shouted over the sound of the crashing waves.

"I don't know, but I'm sure we're gonna' find out." Kyle hated being in the dark, but didn't know what else to do.

"Can we sail out of it?" Kate asked, looking at Kyle as if she expected him to have an answer.

"I can try." Kyle hoped that whatever had driven the boat up to now let him take over the steering. He stumbled his way to the helm of the boat, and grabbed the wheel.

He turned the wheel and the balloon boat responded. He wasn't sure if this was a good thing, since he didn't have much experience with ships, but he was determined to keep them all safe.

He steered the boat to the right. Was that starboard? No.

Wait, yes. Port is to the left. He remembered his father telling him one time that the way to remember the difference is that port had the same amount of letters as left.

The boat responded easily to his direction, but he wasn't fooled that this would be easy. The river was narrower than it had originally looked from above. The edge of the river seemed to fall right off into the space of a trillion twinkling stars. It was beautiful, but it was treacherous.

"Quick Kyle," Ethan shouted. "Go the other way."

Kyle adjusted the wheel to steer to port, but overcompensated and almost took them over that side of the river. He adjusted again, and got the boat back into the middle of the of the raging river. It was a bumpy ride, but he was finally in the right spot.

"Hold tight guys." Kyle had to yell over the noise of the rushing river. "It's getting worse." He could see the rapids in front of them. How was he gong to be able to maintain their course through that, and keep them from sinking?

Huge waves lashed the sides of the boat. The river's turbulence made it difficult for him to hold the boat steady and the deck rose and fell like a ride in an amusement park. Except that this ride wasn't as much fun, and he knew there was no guarantee it would end safely.

Wave after wave pounded the boat mercilessly, and his friends fought to hang on. Kyle watched in horror as a violent wave crashed onto the deck.

Ethan and Mary both disappeared.

# CHAPTER FIFTEEN

"Help!" Ethan's voice was barely audible through the noise of the water. Ethan and Mary were in the river, but Kyle couldn't let go of the wheel or he would lose control of the ship.

Kate couldn't reach them either. She was being thrashed around inside the boat. Kyle watched helplessly as they were carried farther away from the boat by the massive waves.

He could see the terrified expression on Mary's face as she tried to yell, and knew that nothing would come out. A huge wave struck, taking her under, and Kyle screamed.

As if she'd heard him, she surfaced spitting water and gasping. Kyle was momentarily relieved, until he saw Ethan being swept farther away.

They would never be able to reach him.

Kate worked on tying a rope to the boat, and Kyle tried steering closer to Mary without getting too close to the river's edge. Mary went under a second time, and Kyle was sure this time would be her last.

"Someone please help us!" Mary had resurfaced, and Kyle thought he had heard her speak. But that wasn't possible. Mary had never spoken. It had to have been a hallucination on his part.

Kate was yelling for Mary, and preparing to throw the rope when the water began to bubble. A huge head with a golden crown emerged from the center of the bubbles. A beautiful woman, who looked like what Kyle had always imagined as a mermaid floated effortlessly near Mary.

The woman spoke, but Kyle couldn't understand her. She sounded like the dolphins at Sea World when they were giving a show for an audience.

"Help us," Mary said, and this time Kyle heard it for certain. How was that possible? How was Mary suddenly speaking? "We fell overboard."

Kyle glanced at Kate who stared, flabbergasted, watching the scene below her. Which meant that he wasn't the only one who could hear Mary. Either that, or Kate was marveling over the mermaid. Both phenomenons were startling.

The mermaid-woman squeaked again at Mary, and Kyle hoped she was friendly. She didn't look as though she were about to eat Mary, but Kyle didn't know this place.

Kate must not have been sure either, because she yelled again for Mary, and threw the rope toward her.

The mermaid rose higher in the water, and Kyle could see she was actually a very large porpoise. Would he still be able to call her a mermaid? Probably not.

"We have to save Ethan." Mary shouted, and at first Kyle thought she was speaking to Kate. But the porpoise squeaked again, and he realized she and Mary were somehow communicating.

"The water took him," Mary replied to the porpoise.

Kyle could see that Mary was getting tired, even though she was no longer being tossed around by the waves. The porpoise was providing some type of calming element where they were.

"He's out there somewhere." Mary flipped one hand briefly in the direction where Ethan was swept away, then continued to tread water.

The porpoise swam toward Mary. Kyle let go of the wheel and ran to the rail, ready to jump into the water. He saw that Kate already had one leg over and was about to jump as well.

But the porpoise turned to the side, and squeaked at Mary.

Mary, completely unafraid, climbed onto the back of the porpoise. They glided smoothly through the choppy waters and swam quickly over to find Ethan. All Kyle could see of Ethan was his head before he went under water completely.

Mary grabbed Ethan just in time, and managed to help him climb onto the porpoise's back. The porpoise swam easily back to the boat in spite of the still churning waves.

Kyle and Kate hoisted Mary and Ethan back aboard the boat, even as the waves pounded their bodies.

"We need to get them inside, Kate." Kyle didn't want either of them to die of hypothermia or something. He didn't know if the water had been cold enough, but he wasn't going to risk it. Could they get pneumonia after being in the water that long?

"Thank you for rescuing my friends." Kyle wasn't sure the porpoise would be able to understand him, but she seemed to understand Mary. He thought he should at least try to express his gratitude for her saving his friends.

The porpoise squeaked out a replay, so maybe she did understand him. At least in concept? He smiled at her just in case.

Mary, wrapped in a large towel Kate must have found in on of the unexplored cabinets, came to the rail and reached out to the porpoise.

"You saved our lives, Queen Olivia." Mary spoke to the porpoise as if she had been speaking all her life. "I don't know how to thank you."

Kyle had no idea if Queen Olivia was truly the porpoise's name, or if Mary had made it up, but he was so relieved she and Ethan were safe he was willing to call her Queen of the Ocean and Everything In It."

"Mary," Kate said. "You spoke." Kate hugged Mary and they both started laughing.

"I did," Mary exclaimed, and they both began jumping around holding each other. "I can speak."

The boat shifted, reminding them that they weren't out of the storm yet. Kyle looked over at an unusually silent Ethan. He was wrapped in towel similar to Mary's and he was dripping onto the wooden floorboards. He was a mess, but Kyle was still so glad to see him, he hugged him.

Ethan didn't usually go in for physical displays of affection, especially with Kyle, but this time he wrapped his arms around Kyle and hugged him back. Kyle knew this was a testament to how shaken up his dunk in the water had been for him.

The boat began to pick up speed, rocking their group. The water was still rushing dangerously and Kyle ran back to the helm to secure the wheel before they went off course.

"Queen Olivia." Mary turned back to the porpoise who was swimming along side them. "Can you calm the waters?"

Kyle was sure she shook her head, if that's something porpoises can even do, and his heart sank. She squeaked something to Mary, who seemed to understand her, then she swam away.

"Did you understand her?" Kate had been doing the tennis match looks between Mary and Queen Olivia. Kyle would have laughed, but he had been wondering the same question.

"Yes." Mary gave Kate a puzzled look. "Couldn't you?" "All I heard was dolphin noises," Kate replied. "What did she say?"

"She said that she couldn't control the river -- that this is just its way, or something." Mary seemed to consider that for a moment as if processing the meaning. "But then she told me that we're about to land on Terra."

The boat had been moving closer to one of the moons, and Kyle can't help but compare it to a smaller version of Earth.

In the distance he could see the river rising menacingly like a tsunami. It was heading right at them.

# CHAPTER SIXTEEN

"Now would be a good time to go home, Ethan." Kate turned on Ethan and Kyle could see the determination written all over her face. He could tell she'd about maxed out on her patience quota.

Ethan looked at his wrist comm. "I don't see that happening right now." He sounded tired. Kyle hoped it was residual exhaustion from nearly drowning, but was worried it was plain old resignation instead.

"What is it now?" Mary sounded exasperated. Kyle was still getting used to the fact that she could speak at all. It was a nice sound.

The massive wave had finally reached them, so this was no time for anyone to start an argument. "Everybody brace for impact." Kyle shouted, then cranked the wheel hard to the right to try to avoid as much of the wave as possible. At the same time, he prepared for the worst.

A towering wave loomed high above the bow of the boat, then rose out of the water to a height of a three story building. Kyle knew they were all going to drown.

Then he realized it was much worse. The wave morphed into a huge monster with one bulging body, two long necks, two small heads and four red glaring eyes. The 2 heads appeared to be able to move independently from each other. It had what looked like razor sharp teeth, and saliva was gushing from both mouths.

"Kyle," Kate shouted. "Do something!"

"What?" Kyle had never seen anything like this before, and had no idea how to get around it. Did she think he could ram it with the boat? "Look at the size of that thing." It could easily eat the boat for breakfast.

The monster's heads lowered enough that they could see them all hovering in the boat. Both sets of eyes fixed on the group, and Kyle was sure it's next move would be to eat them two at a time.

Kyle had seen <u>Jurassic Park.</u> The best thing to do was stand as still as a statue. His friends must all have thought the same thing, because no one moved an inch.

"Well Wheezey," said the head on the left. "The humans got help from royalty. How clever."

"Yes, Zakery," responded the head on the right. "Very smart indeed."

Kyle was shocked to realize he understood them. He still didn't feel it was safe to move, even if they could talk. But if they could speak, did that mean he could reason with them?

"Are you alright?" asked the one the other had called Zakery. "Sorry, we can sometimes appear terrifying when we first meet someone." He snorted, which Kyle took for laughter. He didn't see the humor in the situation, but was feeling less like they were hostile creatures. "I'm Zakery and this is my twin sister Wheezey. We're the guardians of this moon."

No one spoke, or even moved, so Kyle decided it was up to him to make first contact.

"I'm Kyle." Kyle's voice cracked on the end, and he hoped Kate hadn't heard the nervousness in his voice. He cleared his throat, then gestured to his friends. "This is Ethan, Mary and Kate."

Maybe they wouldn't eat their prey now that they all had names?

"We're happy to meet you Kyle, Ethan, Mary and Kate." The head Zakery had called Wheezey seemed genuinely pleased to be talking to them. That had to be a good sign, right?

"We don't see human's very often," Zakery said. "Where are you from?"

"Ethan's garage." Mary's voice was quiet, and Kyle didn't think she'd meant to be funny, but he stifled a chuckle under his breath. He definitely didn't want to offend these guys, even if they did seem a lot more friendly than he'd expected them to be.

"Ethan's garage," Zakery said, then looked over at his sister in puzzlement. "Never heard of it. How bout' you Wheezey?"

"No, me either," she said, returning Zakery's look. "So why are you here?"

"We're on a mission for Spirit Neal." Kyle hoped that all these strange creatures knew each other. If they knew Spirit Neal had sent them on this quest, maybe they could help.

"Spirit Neal?" Zakery looked even more confused, and Kyle's hopes were dashed. "Never heard of anyone by that name. Sound like anyone you know Wheezey?"

"Nope never heard of him." Wheezey's response only added to Kyle's disappointment."

"We're going to the Kendo kingdom," Kyle explained. "We're on a quest to save the people there from some kind of stone sleep."

"Ahh, yes," Wheezey said, nodding her head. "We have heard about that. Terrible thing to happen."

"But," Zakery said. "You'll need to get passed us and win your reward." He raised his head as if proud of his pronouncement.

"Awww...come on," Kate said, and groaned.

"And if we don't?" Ethan sounded like he was ready to challenge them, and Kyle wanted to throw him back over the rail.

"Then we eat you," replied Wheezey. Which was exactly what Kyle was expecting her to say.

"Think we can take 'em'?" Ethan asked Kate out of the side of his mouth. He thought he was being quiet, but Kyle heard him from twenty feet away at the helm. He was pretty sure the monsters heard him as well. Zakery snorted again.

"Are you out of your mind?" At least Kate was thinking sensibly. But then, she always was the practical one of the siblings. "I say we play along and get outta' here."

"What do we have to do?" Kyle was not willing to risk the siblings getting into one of their arguments while the monsters in front of them might be hungry.

"Just complete one correct answer out of four questions and you can pass." Wheezey smiled like a game show host, and Kyle knew this wasn't going to be nearly as easy as she was making it sound.

"We promise. It's easy." Zakery smiled the exact same smile, and Kyle wanted to turn the boat around and take their chances with the vanishing house. Disappearing for one hundred years sounded better than being eaten alive.

Wheezy bobbed her head in excitement. "Ready for your first question?"

"OK." Kyle wasn't even remotely ready, but there was nothing else they could do except play along.

"If you have me," Wheezey began, "you shouldn't share me.

But if you share me, you've lost me. What am I?"

Kyle turned to his friends, but they all shook their heads and shrugged. All he could do was guess. And if it was the wrong answer, they still had three more chances.

"A pen." Kyle didn't think it was correct, but it was all he could think of.

"Wrong," shouted Weezey. "It's a secret."

"Next question." Zakery jumped right in, giving them no time to register they'd blown their first chance. "What question can never be answered?"

"How high is up?" Mary asked, and everyone looked at her in surprise. "Sorry, did I say that out loud? I'm still not used to having a voice."

"I never heard that one before," Zakery said, then exchanged a look with his sister that said he might have been impressed. "But no. Wrong answer. The answer is 'why'."

Kyle didn't agree with that answer. He believed Mary's answer was better, but before he could even open his mouth to argue, Wheezey was speaking again.

"Ready for your third question?"

"We're running out of questions," Kate said, and Kyle could see the panic beginning to show in her expression. "We have to get this one right."

"What's so weak," Wheezey began, "that speaking breaks it?"

Kyle joins his friends in a circle, and they all stare at each other hoping someone has the answer.

"I think I know this one." Ethan finally broke the silence. "It's rice paper." Kyle thought that sounded ridiculous, but didn't have an answer of is own, so he let it go.

"Wrong." Wheezey crowed in triumph. "It's silence."

Kyle had to admit, that seemed like a much better answer than rice paper, but he was not going to say that to Ethan.

"That's right," Ethan said, and he sounded defeated. "I should have seen that coming. It was so obvious."

It was a more obvious answer, but Kyle could tell that Ethan was being harder on himself than any of the others would have been on him, and didn't say a word. Besides, Kyle hadn't done any better with his response to the first question. "It's okay, Eth." Kate patted Ethan on the back and smiled at him. "We still have one more chance. Fourth times a charm. Right?"

"We'd better prepare to jump overboard just in case." Kyle spoke quietly so that the monsters didn't hear him. His friends all tensed in readiness next to him.

"Here is your final question," Zakery said, completely ignoring them as any threat. "I have lakes, but no water and mountains, but no land. What am I?"

The group returned to their circle and huddled together. "I don't know the answer," Mary said. "Anyone?" She looked at each one individually with hope in her eyes.

"No," Kate replied, sounding defeated. Kyle knew she didn't like not having the correct answers. This was new territory for her. "I don't know."

Zakery's head broke into their circle, and he looked more menacing than he had a few minutes ago.

"Your answer please." Zakery licked his chops, and saliva dripped onto the dark wooden planks of the boat.

"It's..." Kyle stalled for time, but he realized he and his friends were about to be eaten by a monster on another planet. No one would ever know what had happened to them. He was in such a panic, he couldn't even remember the question, let alone come up with an answer.

"A map." Ethan shouted the answer so loud, the entire group jumped back a foot.

"That's right." Zakery pulled his head back to join his sister's. Kyle couldn't tell for sure, but it looked like both heads were disappointed. "You may pass."

The group was elated, and they all gave each other hugs and high-fives. They weren't going to be someone's dinner after all. Kyle felt like they still had a fighting chance to get home.

They were a team. They could do this.

"You'll need this." Wheezey's voice broke into their celebration. She extended her arm and handed Ethan a parchment. "It's a map. It will help you get to your destination faster."

"Thank you." Ethan opened the parchment, and studied it.

Wheezey stretched her head to gaze at the sky. Kyle followed her direction, noticing that the aurora had changed colors again.

"Brother," Wheezey said. "It's time for us to go." "You're right sister." Zakery once again leaned his head into the group. This time he wasn't menacing, but genuinely friendly. "Good luck with your adventure."

"Wait." Kyle realized something that had been gnawing at the back of his mind since the monsters showed up. "How is it we can talk to you? Mary was the only one who could talk with Queen Olivia."

"You can't," replied Wheezey, and she smiled at them showing all over her ferocious teeth. "It's magic."

"Now, wake up," Zakery said.

# CHAPTER SEVENTEEN

Kyle bolted to sitting position, and knocked his head on the bunk above him. For several seconds, he couldn't remember where he was. He searched the room, and realized he was still on the weird balloon boat with his friends, sleeping in the bottom bunk under Ethan's.

Kate and Mary were in the bunks across the room, and Kyle could see through the semi-darkness that they were awake as well.

"Did we just have the same dream?" Kate leaned over the top bunk, checking in on Mary.

"I think so." Mary responded.

"Except that Mary can still speak, so I'm not convinced that was entirely a dream." Kyle knocked on the bunk above him where Ethan was. "Do you have the map?"

Ethan's hand flapped out over the edge of the bunk. He held the map.

"Freaky." Kate seemed more excited than freaked, in Kyle's opinion. "And I'm glad you're still speaking, Mary."

Kate jumped down from her bunk and hugged Mary.

"I hate to break up this love fest." Ethan jumped down from his bunk and stood in the middle of the room. "But..."

He didn't finish his sentence, but it wasn't necessary. Kyle could feel the boat jerk, then speed up. In the dream --or whatever it was -- Queen

Olivia had told them they were approaching Terra. Was the boat anxious to get them there?

Or was the speed for a different reason altogether? What if Wheezey and Zakery decided they would prefer to eat the four of them instead of letting them pass?

Ethan went to the window. Kyle was impressed that Ethan had his sea legs. It was all Kyle, Kate and Mary could do to hold onto something to keep from being tossed around.

The river churned more violently again, and the waters were bashing the boat around like a rubber raft on the white water rapids.

"Everyone hold onto something." Kyle had to shout over the noise of the rushing water.

"Can things get any worse?" Kate sounded more exasperated than afraid, and Kyle was glad to hear it. If Kate was afraid, she wouldn't be able to help them. But Kate exasperated was a powerful force.

"Don't know. Don't care," said Ethan. "I'm scared again." Again? Kyle thought. When was he scared before?

Ethan was never any good at expressing his emotions.

There was the time he won first place at the national science fair, and he acted like it was no big deal. He'd worked for months on his project, so Kyle knew it was a major big deal. But that was Ethan.

"Guys, it just got worse." Mary had joined Ethan at the window, so she and Ethan both knew something that Kyle and Kate hadn't found out yet.

Ethan opened the door and stumbled his way out onto the main deck. Kyle went after him, grabbing onto anything he could find to keep his balance. He didn't want Ethan going over the side again because he was reckless. This time, they might not get him back.

Mary and Kate followed in Kyle's footsteps, and they all assembled on the deck. Kyle went to the helm and could see clearly that this part of the river ended in a vertical drop to the moon.

All four of them screamed as the boat hit the edge of the river, then fell over.

They dropped rapidly, passing through fluffy white clouds. The moon was coming up beneath them fast, and Kyle didn't know how to stop their descent.

Ethan came up behind him, looking green in the face. "Ethan." Kyle shouted to get his attention. "Run the engines full reverse and inflate the balloon to maximum air."

"On it." Ethan seemed determined to keep from throwing up all over the deck. He adjusted the controls, and the balloon immediately began to inflate. It hadn't stopped their fall yet though.

"Now what?" Ethan turned to Kyle, ready for his next instruction.

"You see those valves?" Kyle pointed to a row of valves that looked like the knobs on the old radiators in his parent's house. "Turn them all the way to the left. That should allow more air into the balloon."

Ethan turned all of them as far to the left as they would go. Kyle heard a hissing sound as the balloon filled more quickly. The boat shuttered and everyone grabbed something to keep from being thrown around.

Still, they continued to fall.

# CHAPTER EIGHTEEN

The balloon kept the boat from falling like a rock, but it was still falling. Kyle worried they were too late in filling the balloon, and they were still going to crash. But the descent finally slowed enough that it only skimmed the water, hovering inches above it.

When he was convinced the balloon was keeping them afloat, Kyle focused on their apparent destination. The moon appeared to be similar to Earth. Except that the land on Terra seemed greener, and the water bluer. Kyle wondered if the Earth would still look this brilliant if not for the mess humans had made of it over time.

"I think I left my stomach up there." Ethan's voice broke into Kyle's thoughts and brought him back to their current predicament.

"That's all you left?" Kate asked, and Kyle was relieved she was up to her usual sarcasm.

"How did you know how to do that?" Ethan asked Kyle.

"I don't know," Kyle replied, realizing he truly couldn't explain it. "It just kind of came to me." It had been a thought to him, as if it had always been there waiting to surface.

What if he'd been wrong? Would they have crashed to their death in the waves?

"Over there," shouted Mary. She pointed to distant land in the direction where Kyle had seen the green hills. Kyle adjusted the wheel slightly and steered the balloon boat toward land.

The boat bounced lightly on the shore before settling into the sandy beach and resting. Kyle shut all the valves, and the balloon slowly started to deflate. Then he lowered the gangplank while the others threw on their backpacks. He grabbed his own backpack and all four of them disembarked.

"I'm not doing that again anytime soon." Ethan was beginning to get his normal color back.

Kyle watched as the balloon sank steadily into the boat. He looked up and saw the other two moons orbiting above them.

"I can't get over this place." Kate's voice was barely above a whisper, as if she'd been talking to herself. But Kyle heard her. He seemed to have special hearing when it came to Kate. "I mean, could it get any weirder?"

"I don't see why not." Ethan was nothing if not logical. "Things can always get weirder."

"Ready to go?" Kyle asked. He wanted to keep an argument from starting between the siblings. All he needed was for Kate and Ethan to got at it with each other. Kyle needed the four of them to remember they were a team. They had to work together to get back to Earth and their own time.

"Go where?" Mary asked. She turned in a circle as if looking for an answer to jump out out them.

Ethan pulled out the map and spread it on the ground so that they could all see it.

"It looks pretty straight forward." Kyle wasn't entirely convinced of that, but he had to say something positive to keep up morale. Isn't that what leaders were supposed to do on a constant basis? He placed his finger on the spot on the map for emphasis.

"I think we're here," Kate said, "and it looks like this is where we're going." Her finger traced the line on the map, and ended where Kyle's hand was.

"Should be a path here somewhere." Kyle looked around, much like Mary had done earlier.

"There it is." Mary pointed excitedly in a direction off to the left of where they were huddled.

"Then let's get this movable feast going," Ethan replied while rolling up the map and storing it back in his backpack.

"What does that even mean?" asked Kate, giving Ethan a dubious look.

"Beats me." Ethan shrugged. "I heard it in a movie once." Kyle led the way to the edge of the dense green forest.

There was a definite opening in the trees and a narrow path

that had been cleared. He looked at each of his friends who in turn all nod at him, answering a question he hadn't even asked.

They were ready.

He squared his shoulders and lead the group into the forest. He didn't have a clue as to what they might find inside.

# CHAPTER NINETEEN

The forest was dark and looked ancient.

Kyle couldn't help the feeling that it was alive, brooding and malevolent. The foliage and trees were dense and thick, but he worried about breaking off branches for fear of making the forest angry. Angrier?

They definitely didn't need to make any magical inhabitants angry. They had only just narrowly escaped being eaten. He kept their pace fairly brisk in order to spend as little time as possible in the forest.

Despite their pace, Kyle felt like they had been walking for days. <u>Did this path ever end?</u>

The air was hot and thick with humidity. Kyle could feel his shirt sticking to his back under his backpack. His jeans were molded to his legs, making it harder to walk.

Kyle emerged from the thick trees into an over-grown clearing. They were high enough that the clearing overlooked a lush verdant valley. Just beyond the valley was a mountain with a cascading waterfall.

Kate, Mary and Ethan came up behind him, and he heard Kate gasp over the view. He agreed, it was breathtaking. It was so peaceful, all he wanted to do was lie down and fall asleep for several years.

"We've been walking forever," Mary said. "Can we rest now?"

"No argument here," Ethan said, then moaned. "My legs are killing me."

"Let's stop here." Kyle was relieved he wasn't alone in wanting to call it quits for the day.

The only one who hadn't complained was Kate. Kyle stole a glance in her direction and saw that she had closed her eyes. Was she so tired she'd fallen asleep standing up? Or was she taking in the quiet of the place?

She must have sensed him, because her eyes popped open and she caught him staring at her. He turned abruptly and shook off his backpack. Ethan and Mary had pulled their own backpacks off and were already relaxing, sitting in the grass.

"Hey," shouted Ethan, who jumped back up to his feet. "What's wrong now?" Kate asked, as she, too, shook off her backpack and joined them.

"You didn't see that massive centipede crawl by?" Ethan spun around in circles looking for whatever it was that had startled him.

"No," Kate replied, looking around as well. "I didn't see anything."

"Well I think I'll just stand up for a while." Ethan must have really been spooked by something, because he looked dead on his feet. If he had decided to stay standing, there had to be a good reason, and Kyle wasn't sure he wanted to know what it was.

"Suit yourself." Kate sat down between Kyle and Mary, and the sound of her stomach growling made her blush.

"Someone's hungry." Mary smiled at Kate, then nudged her teasingly with her shoulder.

"I was, too," Ethan said. "Until I saw that thing crawl by."

"Well I'm hungry," Kyle said. "I'm gonna' eat." He didn't care what Ethan had seen, Kyle was hungry enough to eat Wheezey and Zakery combined.

They all rummaged through their backpacks and produced sandwiches, fruit, and various snacks. Kyle was impressed. Neal must have stocked them up before they left the house. Would their food supply run out eventually? Or did Neal's power extend to wherever they were?

Ethan, apparently drawn in by the sight of all the delicious food, decided he would rather eat than worry about a giant centipede that might, or might not, have been a product of his over-active imagination.

"So what's the plan?" Ethan asked through mouthfuls of sandwich.

Kyle waited to swallow his bite of fruit before responding, hoping Ethan would take the hint. But it wasn't very likely. There was no getting around it -- Ethan was brilliant, but he was a total slob.

"According to Spirit Neal, we grab the fire flowers," said Kyle, "and give them to someone called the Old Guard. They do their thing to bring everyone back, our mission is finished, and then we go home."

"We hope," said Kate. She didn't talk with her mouth full, Kyle noticed. But he also noticed that she sounded particularly pessimistic, which was a bit out of the norm for Kate.

"Well, it sounds like a good plan to me." Mary was always optimistic. And since she had started to speak, her levels of hopefulness seemed to have gone even higher.

"I kind of want to stay a while," said Ethan, "and learn more about this world."

"Uh-huh," responded Kate. "Good luck with that."

Kyle rolled his eyes. Why didn't it surprise him that Ethan was thinking more about exploring this strange place instead of wanting to get back home? It was Ethan's way. Kyle supposed that it might be an interesting place to explore if they had more of a guarantee they would all be returned safely back home afterward.

He grabbed the map out of Ethan's backpack and checked it to see where they were.

"I think we're close." He took a moment to acclimate their position on the map again, but it still looked correct. Taking into account he was reading the map the right way, Kendo Kingdom should be close. "It should be around here some place."

He turned to ask Ethan a question, but noticed a glint of light in the direction beyond where Ethan was sitting.

"Hey, look at that." Kyle leaned forward and pointed it out. In the distance he could see a large dome-shaped glass building reflecting the sun light.

"Wow," said Mary, and she leaned forward to get a better look.

"We should check it out." Ethan was excited, as if his wish to explore had come true.

They hastily shoved the remnants of their lunch back into their backpacks, slung them over their respective shoulders, and headed toward the dome. It seemed that they were all excited, because Kyle hadn't seen the group move this quickly since they'd arrived here.

This time Ethan lead the way, but Kyle was fine with that. He'd bring up the rear and keep an eye on things. Ethan had a tendency to get laser-focused when he was set on something. Kyle knew it was his responsibility to watch out for things when Ethan got that way.

And Kyle was convinced this wasn't going to be as easy as Ethan was making it seem. Nothing on this planet was turning out to be what they expected.

# CHAPTER TWENTY

The domed building was a mess.

Kyle was disappointed to see that the glass in the windows was discolored and cracked. There was some kind of vined plant growing up the outside of the building and the old wooden door was weathered and splintered.

A large Calico cat scurried up to them, then hopped up onto an old stone block next to the door. He sat there swishing his tail and watched them. Kyle felt like the cat was waiting for something. A treat? Maybe he should share some of his sandwich with the cat? Would it be a friendly cat?

"It looks like no one's been here for ages." Kate went to one of the windows and peered inside. She rubbed one of the panes with her sleeve, but it must not have made any difference because she gave up and rejoined the group.

"Yeah," Kyle responded, keeping one eye on the cat in case it wasn't friendly. "I wonder why?"

"It must've been really amazing once." Kate sounded wistful.

Kyle smiled. Kate loved history.

"Look at that cat." Mary walked over to the cat to get a better look. "He's so big."

"That is a big cat." Ethan barely glanced at the cat, intent on figuring a way into the building. Kyle knew that in about three minutes, Ethan wouldn't even remember there was a cat.

Mary carefully held out her hand to the cat. "Hello there," she said in a gentle voice. "What's your name?"

The cat stood on all four legs its eyes widened in surprise. "You can talk?"

Mary took a step back, and everyone stared at the cat in shock. Even Ethan stopped his inspection and took notice of the talking cat.

"I don't get to speak to humans much," the cat continued speaking. "In fact, not since the war."

Kyle hoped the cat wasn't getting ready to pounce, and moved closer to Mary to be be ready to grab it if it launched.

"I see you're wearing a choker like mine." Mary spoke to the cat, and pointed to the collar around its neck. "This necklace makes it possible for me to speak to animals, so perhaps that's why we can understand you, too."

"Wait 'til I tell my pride I spoke to a human." The cat seemed to puff up at the thought. "They'll say, 'No you didn't.' And I'll say, 'Yes I did.' And then they'll say, 'No, you didn't.' And then I'll say, 'Yes, I did.' Then they'll say, 'No --'"

"Excuse me," Mary said, interrupting the cat before it could continue on forever in its imaginary debate, "but I was wondering... Can you tel me where we are?"

"Your right here, of course." The cat eyed Mary as if it questioned her intelligence. Kyle snorted a laugh. The cat was a smart aleck. He was going to like this cat.

"This is the Kendo Kingdom," said the cat when Mary continued to stare at it. "A wonderful and magical place where anything can happen."

"Is it safe to go into the dome?" Kyle wanted to be sure they wouldn't be hurt if they did find a way inside.

"Of course," replied the cat. "I go in there all the time. There's no food though, since the human's stopped coming."

Kyle didn't like the sound of that. Why would people stop coming?

"So, who are you?" the cat asked Mary. "I've never seen you here before."

"Oh," replied Mary, as if embarrassed that she'd forgotten her manners when meeting a cat. "My name is Mary."

"Maaaaaaarrryyyy." The cat practically purred Mary's name, and Kyle thought it sounded musical.

"Yes, that's it." Mary giggled, making Kyle believe she had liked the sound as well. "These are my friends, Kyle, Ethan and Kate."

She pointed to each of them in turn and the cat followed her gestures with its bright brown eyes. It purred, then asked, "They're part of your pride, then?"

"Yes, I guess we are a pride." Mary smiled at the others. "Then they are okay with me, Maarrry." The cat purred then nodded in affirmation.

"You're getting better with my name." Mary turned her brilliant smile on the cat, who purred again.

"We have to go." Kyle whispered the words, reluctant to break up the new friendship between Mary and the cat. "The sun's setting, and we need to find a place to camp."

"We have to go now," Mary said to the cat. "I hope we'll see you again."

"May I come with you, Maarrry?"

"Sure." Mary shrugged. "I don't see why not."

"I'll meet you inside then." The cat jumped down then shouted down the street. "Hey guys. Hey! You'll never guess what I've been doing."

Kyle watched as the cat met up with a group of other cats. He looked distinctly haughty, and then Kyle heard, "Maarrry."

"Oh, great," Ethan said, and groaned. "Another mouth to feed."

"Remember," Mary said, pointing her finger at Ethan like she's scolding a student for talking too loud in the library. "We're the strangers here."

Kyle couldn't help but laugh. Mary being able to speak was going to be so much fun. "Okay, let's go inside."

# CHAPTER TWENTY-ONE

They all stood at the front door, glancing at each other.

No one made a move to go inside.

All three heads finally shifted to Kyle, and he realized he was going to have to lead the way, or they would be standing out here until they all grew old.

Kyle sighed, then took a deep breath psyching himself up for the unknown. He opened the door a crack and peered inside.

The sun filtered through the top of grimy glass dome. More of the same vines from the outside had made their way along the walls on the inside. Overgrown grass spread wildly through the cracks in the stone floor, and moss covered the ancient wooden walls.

In the middle of the round room was a large, oval-shaped clearing set into the stone floor. There were marble chairs arranged around one side of the oval.

Kyle half expected several members of royalty to come out, sit down, and ask why he and his friends were there. But the chairs remained as empty as the rest of the room.

He opened the door all the way, and the whole group cautiously entered the domed building. Kyle moved further into the room and saw gray stone statues scattered everywhere. Some of the statues were broken and covered with the same grass and mold from the floor and the walls.

"Some kind of recreation or lounge area maybe?" Ethan's voice boomed through the silence of the room, echoing around the group and Kyle nearly screamed.

"Looks like it." Kyle responded, as soon as his heartbeat had returned to normal. He spoke quietly to make it clear he didn't have to shout to be heard.

"It must have been beautiful." Kate took Kyle's cue and kept her voice low as well.

"What do you think happened?" asked Mary.

Kate leaned low over a statue of a female who's arm and head were missing, then said, "A terrible battle of some kind?"

"The cat said they used to use this room a lot at one time." Mary reminded them. "He didn't say what happened. He was very fascinated about us though."

Kyle examined a statue near him of a man who had pulled his sword before falling. All that was left of the sword in his hand was the ornate hilt. "Who were they fighting," Kyle asked. "And why?"

Ethan moved over to a set of double doors on the far side of the room that was partially covered behind a wall. The cat had wandered in through the open front door, and followed Ethan to the double doors.

"Guys," Ethan said. He'd shouted again, but this time Kyle was more prepared. "Check this out."

Kyle, Kate and Mary made their way to the doors as Ethan examined two tarnished brass ring handles.

"The entrance to the Kendo Kingdom," said the cat, and a shiver ran down Kyle's spine. Was the cat deliberately trying to scare them?

The knobs were very old and clearly hadn't been used in a long time, if the vines encircling them were any indication.

Ethan yanked on the handle, but it didn't move. "They're stuck." Ethan yanked again, then started pounding on the doors.

Kyle wasn't sure what Ethan hoped to gain by pounding on the doors. If there were people -- or whatever -- on the other side to open the doors, would they be friendly? Or would they be more monsters wanting to eat them?

Or worse, would they be the thing that had made all these people crazy, then turned them to stone?

"I think," said Mary, "if we move all this stuff away we might be able to open it.

They each took a section of the vines and tore away anything that looked like it was blocking the doors and the handles.

"Okay, let's try now." Kyle stood back and waited for Ethan to try the handles again.

Ethan yanked on the handles again, but nothing happened. Kyle grabbed the handle next to the one Ethan was pulling, and they pulled together.

Still, nothing happened. Kate joined Kyle, and Mary joined Ethan, and together for four of them pulled.

Slowly, with some resistance, the doors finally began to creak open.

# CHAPTER TWENTY-TWO

"I can't see," Kate said. "It's too dark." Her voice was barely above a whisper. A stark contrast to the level of noise her brother was making.

Ethan was banging around, shrugging out of his backpack.

He pulled the crystal ball from its sack, then held it up. "Light our way." Ethan's command was loud enough to be heard back on Earth. Kyle was convinced Ethan got a perverse pleasure out of ordering something to do whatever he wanted.

The crystal ball sparked instantly, glowing like a torch to illuminate the tunnel. The light reflected off of water dripping down the stone walls, reminding Kyle of one of those creepy movies his parents liked to watch in black and white. The sound echoed faintly around them, only adding to the spooky ambiance.

Directly ahead of the group were well-worn steps that descended into the inky blackness below.

"Ethan, you have the light," Kyle said. "You take the lead."

Ethan stepped carefully past Kyle and started the group down the stairs. They went slowly in single file until their steps ran out and they reached the bottom.

Just in front of Ethan, Kyle could see an opening to what looked like a dusty tunnel. As they got closer, he could see old torches hanging from the walls.

Kyle reached for a torch, then nearly dropped it when it flared to life on its own. The light revealed a long, gloomy tunnel that didn't exactly give Kyle the welcoming he was hoping for.

Mary and Kate both grabbed torches, and weren't nearly as shocked as Kyle had been when they, too, flared with light on their own. Ethan stowed the crystal ball back into its home in his backpack, then picked up his own torch and watched it light itself.

"I wonder how far this thing goes?" Kate raised her torch to see if she could get a better look, but Kyle had already tried that. There was no end in sight.

"Probably all the way to Middle Earth." Ethan must be nervous. His snark level had gone up drastically.

"Be serious Ethan." Kyle was nervous, too, and Ethan was not helping the situation.

"I am," Ethan replied, and Kyle wanted to punch him.

He decided it was safer talking to Mary. "Do you remember if the cat said anything about this tunnel?"

"Hey." Mary turned around. "Where is he?"

"I thought he was right behind us." Kate went to the stairs, waved her torch, and searched for the cat.

"Apparently not," Ethan said, pointing out the obvious.

Seriously, tensions were already high. Ethan being a jerk wasn't helping the situation. He was getting on Kyle's last nerve.

"Well, now that we've established that." Kate didn't sound like she appreciated Ethan's sarcasm any more than Kyle had. "Can we get moving? This place is starting to creep me out."

"Right, let's see where this thing goes." Kyle didn't particularly want to find out, but he knew they were going to have to get moving whether he liked it or not. Since Ethan was apparently done being the "fearless" part of their leader, Kyle took over the front once more.

The tunnel curved left and then right, and Kyle hoped they wouldn't have to take the same way back out again. If they had to come back this way, he would probably get them hopelessly lost.

After what seemed like years, he finally saw a sliver of light up ahead. He was relieved to see what was left of the day's light at the end of the tunnel. He was so glad the sun hadn't completely set while they were wandering around in there. It meant that they couldn't have been in there for more than a few hours.

Apparently, the rest of them were as anxious to get out of the tunnel as he was, because they all broke into a run to reach the opening.

"Finally," Ethan said on a sigh. "I didn't think we'd ever get out of there."

"We know," Mary said, and she didn't look happy. "You kept complaining the whole time."

Kyle was glad to hear Mary saying something that wasn't her normal optimistic and positive self. He was also glad it had been directed at Ethan and not at himself. You had to work really hard to put Mary in a bad mood. Or, you just had to be Ethan.

"Someone had to do it." Ethan grinned, like he'd had an important role in keeping morale up.

Again, Kyle wanted to punch him. From the looks on their faces, Kate and Mary would have been willing to hold Ethan down for him.

They'd reached the opening in the tunnel, and all four of them stood there stunned and gaping.

The kingdom was run down. It looked as though it had been through some kind of disaster or devastating event. Either that, or its inhabitants were incredibly careless with their upkeep.

Dragons and birds flew through the sky. One dragon rested in the open square. The streetlights are beginning to light just like their torches in the tunnel. They seemed surprisingly bright considering what a wreck the kingdom was.

Kyle couldn't help but be disappointed in what he saw. He had expected so much more from a place that called itself a "kingdom."

The cat jumped down from somewhere above them and startled everyone. Ethan let out a short scream, and Kyle had to hold back a laugh. Ethan would never forgive him if he laughed at him in front of Mary and Kate.

"Hello again." Mary was the first to catch her breath. "How did you get here before us?"

"There are many ways into Kendo Kingdom," the cat replied. Was it Kyle's imagination, or had the cat seemed shifty when he said that? He wondered what secrets this cat was hiding.

# CHAPTER TWENTY-THREE

"This is a magical kingdom," the cat said, then turned and began walking away. "Follow me."

Kyle didn't think they should be following some stray cat. However, since no one else came up with any better ideas, himself included, they all followed the cat.

The kingdom resembled a crumbling 17th century European city with ancient stone houses and walls.

"Something really bad happened here." Kyle couldn't shake the feeling of despair as they wandered through the streets of broken roads and collapsing homes.

"I never really understood," said the cat, murmuring to himself, "why human's do what they do."

Again, Kyle stared at the cat, and wondered what was going on inside that furry, somewhat creepy, brain. That cat was hiding something. It was strange how it constantly referred to its interactions with humans as if they had happened in a distant past.

Kyle was about to ask the cat directly about it when Mary said, "We don't understand it either."

While that was true in Kyle's opinion as well, he didn't think Mary should be admitting to human failures in front of the cat. Cats definitely did not need more reason to feel superior.

"I can't believe dragons really do exist." Kate's gaze was focused on the sky, watching as several dragons flew overhead.

Kyle spied a dragon sleeping in the open square. As if sensing Kyle's gaze, the dragon woke, lifted its massive blue-scaled head, and watched them through large brown eyes the color of melted caramel. Kyle continued to watch as the majestic animal shifted its position, sniffed the air, then laid its head back down to continue his slumber.

"I wonder if we can ride them?" Ethan asked, but Kyle noticed his voice wasn't nearly as loud as he usually projected. He glanced at Ethan and could see that he was as in awe of the dragons as the rest of them. "I've ridden horses before. It can't be that different. Right?"

Ethan turned to Kyle as if expecting some sort of confirmation. Kyle had no idea if dragons would let them ride them. He shrugged, hoping that would be the end of it, because he preferred not to ride a dragon. That sounded like something that would definitely end in their deaths.

"Yeah," said Mary, "except horses don't fly."

Mary was being sensible, too, and Kyle was relieved he wasn't the only one who was thinking that riding dragons would be a dumb idea.

"They don't eat you either." Good, Kate was also on the Don't Ride Dragons team.

"You can only ride them if they let you." The cat's voice startled Kyle who had forgotten it was even there. Well, that and he was also still trying to get used to a talking cat. "They are a proud and intelligent race," continued the cat, "and they must be respected."

Fine. Kyle had no problem respecting them. Especially from a distance. And on the ground.

Dragons were huge. Kate's comment about dragons eating humans was still hanging in the air. They didn't know anything about dragons, not in real life. All he knew was what he'd read in books. And who knew how accurate that was?

The people they passed seemed beaten and defeated, slumped in the shoulders and heads bowed. None of them even glance at Kyle or the group as they made their way through the town.

"They all look so sad." Mary sounded as if she was on the verge of crying herself.

"Many of them lost loved ones to stone." The cat sounded angry. "These are the survivors."

Kyle wondered why the cat would be angry. Was it angry because they were all suffering? Or angry because there were still survivors. He didn't know why, but he wasn't sure he trusted the talking cat. There was something suspicious about how it kept following them around.

A few more paces up the street, Kyle noticed that some of the stone people and dragons strewn along the path were broken. Had they been smashed? Or had they fallen?

"These were once alive?" Kate sounded both appalled and disturbed at the same time.

"Yes," said the cat. It didn't say anything more, and that made Kyle even more suspicious.

The group continued to make their way through the old streets. Kate turned in circles as she walked as if wanting to be sure she didn't miss anything from any angle.

In the distance Kyle spied a castle on a hill, and hoped that its inhabitants were at least friendly. He saw, even from this distance, that the building had seen better days. It looked like it had been beaten. There were holes in place of the windows, and the front doors had been knocked off their hinges.

"Hey guys," Kate said, causing Kyle to take his mind and eyes off the castle and turn her way. "We've got company."

She was walking backward, which meant someone was approaching from behind them. Kyle whipped around to see a tall black man dressed as some kind of palace guard. He was probably in his late sixties, and he looked exactly like--.

"Mr. Aaron?" Kyle could not believe their teacher was here.

"I'm known by many names," replied the Mr. Aaron look-alike, "but I'm not familiar with that one."

"Sorry you look like--" Kyle felt stupid. Of course their teacher wasn't here. He hadn't been with them in the garage when everything went nuts. But for a brief moment, Kyle had thought their mentor had come to rescue them, and that had been such a relief.

"Cat!" The old guard sparked an interest in seeing the cat with them. "Where have you been my old friend?"

# CHAPTER TWENTY-FOUR

How did the cat know Mr. Aaron?

Kyle mentally smacked himself for being a dope. Cat --which is what the guard-man had called the cat -- didn't know Mr. Aaron. This guy wasn't Mr. Aaron. He looked like Mr.

Aaron, and talked like Mr. Aaron, but this was a completely different world.

This man was not Mr. Aaron.

Kyle had to keep reminding himself that they were not anywhere near their own world anymore.

"After the war," Cat said, as it wondered closer to the guard, "I joined my pride and never looked back."

"How is it possible we can talk with and understand the animals here?" Mary asked.

Kyle realized that she must still be getting used to being able to speak at all. How strange it must have been for her, to miraculously be able to speak after fifteen years. And then to discover she can also speak with the animals in this world? It was strange enough in Kyle's mind, so she must really be blown away.

"The magic of this place makes it possible," the guard answered. "I don't pretend to know how, it just is."

"Can I talk to the dragons too?" Apparently, Ethan was still hung up on the dragons.

"Yes," said the guard, turning to speak directly to Ethan. "As long as you respect them." He gave Ethan a quizzical stare. "You are not from here."

"No," Kyle said, cutting into the conversation before Ethan could say something stupid. He was afraid one of them might give too much information about where they came from and how they got to this place. He didn't know if they could trust this Mr. Aaron look-alike. The only people Kyle knew he could trust were his friends. "We're from far away."

"Then welcome to the Kendo Kingdom." The guard smiled at the group, but Kyle could tell there wasn't as much heart in the smile as there once might have been when he was welcoming people to this kingdom. "It's rare we see visitors since the war."

Someone's stomach growled loudly. Kyle was pretty sure it had been his own. They hadn't eaten since their snack, and their hunger was catching up with all of them.

"I'm sorry," the guard said. "Have you eaten? Do you have somewhere to stay tonight?"

"No to both questions." Ethan informed the guard, who smiled again at them. This time in pity.

"It's late." The guard stated. "Come, stay with me. It's not much, but I can provide a roof over your heads and a warm meal. Cat and I have much catching up to do."

"Thank you," Kyle said, accepting the invitation on behalf of the whole group. "That's very kind." He still didn't know if he could trust the man, but it was a generous offer.

Who knew when they would get another one?

Spirit Neal had told them to find the Old Guard. This man certainly looked like an old guard. Then again, what made him think they could trust Spirit Neal either? This whole quest could be leading all of them to a very bad end.

The old guard lead them through a few winding streets off the main road, and they followed him in single file. Cat jumped from spot to spot keeping up with them along the way.

They passed more battered or destroyed homes. Some were made of wood, and some of stone, but none of them had escaped the destruction.

"What happened to your kingdom?" Kyle asked the guard hoping he would get better information than they had from Cat, who had only made vague references to a war.

"It's a long story," the guard replied, and let out a heavy sigh. "Many suffered. Come, my home is just this way."

His home sat at the end of a street tucked away off the main part of the town. It appeared to have missed the fighting, and had remained intact. The house was small, but seemed clean and neat.

The guard opened his front door and gestured them all inside. There was a small couch that sat in front of a fireplace where a warm fire was already blazing. Beyond the couch was a table with four chairs in front of a wooden cupboard.

Moonlight filtered through wooden window shutters, and Kyle realized that they must have walked much longer than he had imagined.

Well-worn battle gear hung on the walls including an archer's bow, two swords and a large black cape. None of the objects looked particularly special in any way, but there was something about each one that drew his attention.

Kyle had always been fascinated by ancient weapons. He had no idea if these were historical decoration, or of the guard had used them just yesterday, but they appeared to be kept in good condition. As if the guard was waiting for something to happen that would require him to use them at a moment's notice.

The guard made his way around the room lighting several candles and set a few on the table. He motioned for the group to sit, then added two more chairs for himself and for Cat.

"It still looks the same." Cat said, then hopped up onto one of the empty chairs. It seemed strange to Kyle for a cat to join them at the table, but Cat acted so at home here, Kyle shrugged off his bias and decided to go with the flow.

"This house has been through a lot." The old guard seemed lost in his thoughts. From the look on his face, Kyle didn't think the thoughts were happy memories.

"What happened?" Kyle didn't want to intrude, but they needed all the information they could get if they were all going to survive this quest.

"We fought against Warren, the evil King of Shumary." The guard sat up straighter, proud of his role. "He put a spell on our Kingdom that turned people to stone. Including our King."

"It was bad," said Cat, agreeing with the guard. "That's terrible." Mary's voice was barely above a whisper, but Kyle still heard the deep sadness in it, and felt the same way.

"Is there a way to break the spell?" Ethan asked.

"North of here is King Warren's lair." The old guard gestured vaguely in a direction Kyle could only assume was North. "He possesses a field of magic fire flowers that will break the spell. But he'll never relinquish them and they're fiercely guarded."

"Has anyone tried to get them?" Kyle realized that was probably a stupid question, and half expected the guard to tell him that no question was stupid, just like Mr. Aaron would say.

"Many have," said the guard, nodding his head. "But none have succeeded."

"Judging by your gear," said Kyle, pointing at all the weapons on the wall, "it looks like you fought in the battle too."

"I'm an expert swordsman and martial fighter," replied the guard, barely giving his own weapons a glance. "I was our King's right hand officer before being defeated in the war."

The room went silent and Kyle suspected, like him, they were all giving the guard a moment to himself to grieve his losses. It must have been hard to have been someone so important once, to end up so lost and all alone.

Kyle wouldn't let anything like that happen to his friends.

Ethan broke the melancholic mood by rummaging in his bag.

He held up the crystal ball and loudly stated, "Show me what happened in the Kendo Kingdom." He seemed so proud of his idea and his new toy.

# CHAPTER TWENTY-FIVE

The crystal ball began to glow casting brilliant light around the dimly lit room. Clouds swirled, reminding Kyle of time passing backward in a Sci-Fi movie. The room filled with a three dimensional holographic image of the town.

"Magic," said the Cat, sounding mystified.

"I have seen this magic before," said the old guard. He sounded as if he couldn't quite remember where, which Kyle thought was strange. Wasn't the whole kingdom magic?

The image loses its fuzziness, focusing in on the Kendo Kingdom/ But it wasn't the same Kendo Kingdom where they were. This one was bustling, the streets are full of people. Vendors in the streets selling their goods mingled with the people who lived there. The colors were bright and flashy, and the people appeared busy and happy.

The same castle Kyle had seen earlier sat on the hill and glowed in the sunlight. The windows all gleamed with glass, and the front door was wide open and welcoming.

"It was a sunny day." Ethan's voice droned, making him sound like he was in a trance. "The people were out doing their chores, shopping in the square and conversing. They didn't know just outside the Kingdom a large well-armed army approached, lead by King Warren."

"We were about to celebrate the kingdoms birthday." The old guard spoke no louder than a whisper, as if not wanting to break Ethan's trance. "Instead, it turned into a bloodbath."

Kyle leaned in closer to the holographic image and watched as King Warren and his men, dressed in full battle gear, positioned themselves along the main entry to the kingdom.

"King Warren of Shumary," Ethan continued, "demanded that the king of Kendo hand over the kingdom to him. When the king of Kendo refused, King Warren ordered his army to attack the people of Kendo."

The group watched the image in horror as King Warren and his army descended upon the kingdom, slashing and killing everyone and everything within their reach. The king of Kendo, protected by the royal guard, hid his family in secret passages in the palace. Then he took up arms with his guards to meet King Warren.

"For days," Ethan spoke again, "King Warren sent his men to the Kendo Kingdom. Both armies fought, the scene was nightmarish. Kendo soldiers died in the city streets."

The image showed soldiers being cut down by King Warren's army. People in the streets ran for cover, but were still caught and killed.

"Lighting cracked from the sky striking people, dragons and the entire royal family." Ethan's voice continued to drone. "A spell had been cast on them, turning almost everyone to stone."

People were turned to stone, frozen in mid-flight, while others ran screaming and searching for cover from the lightning.

And Ethan continued his grisly monologue. "King Warren's soldiers smashed the statues of everyone they found. The fallen flags of the Kendo Kingdom lay on the blood and rubble that filled the streets."

When Kyle was sure he couldn't watch any longer, the image faded and the crystal ball returned to normal.

The group sat in silence. Kyle felt sick to his stomach.

Who was this horrible King Warren? How could he be so evil?

Ethan was dazed after the conjuring, and Kyle could tell it was going to take him several minutes to get over whatever it was he went through when channeling -- or whatever that was -- with the crystal ball.

They were all too stunned to say anything, but Kyle felt compelled to try. "We can help you. We'll get the fire flowers and bring them back to free your kingdom."

"Thank you, my boy," said the guard, and he reached out and patted Kyle's hand. "But I would not ask you to do such a difficult task. To risk your lives to find something that is only a legend for my kingdom is wrong. No. We will fight King Warren and one day we will defeat him and break the spell."

"But we want to do it." Mary sounded as desperate as Kyle felt. "We have gifts that will help us. You have to let us try."

The old guard smiled, but it was an indulgent smile. "I assure you the people of the Kendo Kingdom will someday be victorious."

"But what if that day is now?" Kyle wanted the guard to take them seriously. Mr. Aaron wouldn't have dismissed them so easily.

They all stared at the old guard, who looked like he was at least considering it. Neither Ethan nor Kate had spoken up yet, but Kyle knew they would stay with the group. They were a team. They always had been. They always would be.

"I noticed you appreciate fine armaments." The guard stood up from his chair and went over to the wall full of weapons. "Are you a warrior?"

"Yes, in a way," Kyle replied. "I was a football player in high school, which is kind of like a warrior."

The old guard began removing pieces from his collection of weapons from the wall.

"I want you to have these things," he said, as he reverently brushed his hands along one of the swords. "They brought me status and protection."

He stretched his arms holding the sword out to Kyle. Kyle could only gape at the guard, unsure of what he was doing. Was the man giving Kyle his sword? How could he accept such a gift?

"This is the Sword of Fire and Ice." The guard laid the sword gently in Kyle's hands. "It can be activated by simply thinking about it, but it can only be used in battle. Beware though: The more intense your emotions, the more intense the power of the sword."

Kyle was speechless. He didn't know what to say to the guard, to thank him for such a miraculous gift.

Before he could say anything to him, the guard picked up an archer's bow, and handed it to Mary.

"This is a special archers bow," the guard said. "To shoot it, pull back on it and an exploding arrow will appear. This is the only weapon that can be used anytime."

"This strap," continued the guard, helping Mary adjust a leather strap across her back, "goes on like this so you can carry it on your back."

Mary maneuvered the strap more comfortably over her back, and examined the bow more closely.

The guard reached for another sword in his collection and took it down from the wall. It was slightly smaller and thinner than the one he'd given to Kyle, but both had obviously been created by the same master craftsman.

"This is the sword of light," said the guard, and he handed it to Kate. "Point it and wave it in a narrow arch at your opponents. The sword throws out white light erasing everything in its path. Again, it can only be used during battle. Same as the Sword of Fire and Ice, it is only a sword when not in battle."

Kyle had a brief moment to wonder when using a sword wasn't a battle. Did it matter whether it was against one person or hundreds? But he didn't to break the mood by voicing his question. He would just have to trust that the magic knew the difference even if he didn't.

Kate tried lifting the sword into the air, but it must have been heavier than it looked because she stumbled to keep her balance. She made a few practice swings, but was clumsy in wielding it.

Kyle knew she wouldn't let its weight deter her. When Kate put her mind to something, she would get it done.

"It's heavy." Kate huffed out a breath, but Kyle could see the determination in her face.

"The more you use it," the guard explained, "the lighter it becomes. Soon it will be as easy to wield as your right hand."

Kate nodded then used both hands, handling it better with each swing.

"You will also need the Cape of Cover," said the guard, expertly dodging one of Kate's wild swings. He handed her the plain black cloak. "Hold it high above you and it creates a magical shield around you and those near you. You will be protected from man and earth.

"These are amazing," said Kate, still practicing her sword moves. "Thank you."

Kyle swung his sword a few times to test it out like Kate was doing. He felt powerful, like a true warrior. But they were too important to be given away. "These are priceless possessions. We can't possibly accept them."

"I gift them to you," said the guard, "to protect you on your journey and in battle. The warrior spirit is powerful in all of you. It cannot be stilled."

"Ahem," Ethan said, clearing his throat as an interruption. "Where's my cool thing?"

Kyle was embarrassed by Ethan's spoiled attitude, and wanted to shake him. Ethan was a great friend, with a brilliant mind, but he really didn't know how to read a room.

"You have what you need already," said the guard, effectively putting Ethan in his place without too much fuss. Then he yawned loudly, and Kyle heard the man's jaw crack. "Forgive me. This old body needs rest. I'll see you all in the morning."

He picked up a candle from the table and started toward the back of the house. "Or perhaps not..."

# CHAPTER TWENTY-SIX

"Ethan," Kyle whispered, "we'll be leaving before sunrise. Stop whining about it."

After the guard left, the group laid out their sleeping bags around the fire and settled in for the night. No sooner had they all settled into their bags, Ethan began grumbling. He didn't like the idea of getting up before dawn to get an early start.

"What's wrong with after sunrise?" Ethan's voice whispered back in the dark.

"I want to go before he wakes up," Kyle said, still whispering. "Try to get some sleep."

"Are you kidding?" Ethan sat up and glared at Kyle. "It's too early I'll never get to sleep."

"Well, we're going at Sunrise either way, so stay up all night if you want." Kyle's whisper sounded more forceful than he'd intended, but Ethan's spoiled two-year-old act was making him angry.

"No," said Ethan, not bothering to whisper anymore. "I'm waiting till morning. You can go without me."

"Shhh." Kyle was sure the guard had to be able to hear them arguing. "Keep your voice down."

"You have to go, Ethan. You're important to us," Kate's voice whispered over to them through the dark.

"Kyle doesn't think so," Ethan said, not bothering to whisper any longer. Even in the dark Kyle could hear the pout in Ethan's voice. "Not the way he treats me."

"What do you mean the way I treat you?" Kyle's whisper raised up a notch in volume. Why was Ethan being such a jerk? "We're like family. Especially now, when we're all we have. We have to stay together."

"Look we're all tired and on edge," Kate said, trying to keep the peace. "Why don't we get some sleep and hash it out in the morning."

"There's nothing to hash out," Ethan said. "I'm not going."

Kyle heard rustling, and felt Ethan moving around next to him. Then he saw a shadowy figure on the other side of the room, and knew that Ethan had moved his sleeping bag to be faraway from the group.

He was going to be cold over there so far away from the fire, but Kyle wasn't going to point that out. Not with the mood Etan was in. If he wanted to be a jerk, he could be a jerk on his own side of the room.

He hoped Ethan would sleep off his tantrum in time for them to leave in the morning. The last thing he wanted was for the group to split up. It took him several minutes to calm down, but eventually he felt sleep drag him under.

The next thing he knew, it was close to dawn and the fire had almost gone completely out. It was chilly in the room, but the sleeping bag kept him warm. He didn't want to leave his warm spot, but he knew they had to get a move on if they wanted to get an early start on their journey.

He rolled over and noticed that he had been right last night. Ethan had gone over to the other side of the room to sleep by himself. Kyle rolled his eyes, then decided to let it go.

He crawled out of his sleeping bag and went over to wake Kate and Mary. Kate was closest, and he took a moment to see how peaceful she was in her sleep. She slept with one hand under her chin as if, even in sleep, she was constantly thinking.

He smiled at her, then shook his head. What was wrong with him, watching Kate sleep? Creepy much?

"Hey, Kate." Kyle whispered loudly, then reached over and shook her awake. "Wake up."

"Huh?" Kate opened her eyes, then stretched. "It's morning?"

"Shhhh..." Kyle resisted the urge to cover her mouth. "You'll wake up the Old Guard. We need to get going."

Cat, who had been sleeping on the small couch, woke up and stretched a long feline stretch.

"I'm hungry," said Mary, who was sitting up and rubbing her eyes. "How about breakfast?"

"We'll eat on the trail," Kyle replied. He really wanted to get going before the old guard woke up. He wasn't trying to sneak out on the old guard, or deceive him in any way, but he also didn't want the old man to try to stop them either.

Cat licked its paws as the group folded up their sleeping bags and got all their things together. Everyone except Ethan. "Are you coming Ethan?" Kate glared at her brother, hands

on her hips, and waited for him to get out of his sleeping bag.

"No," Ethan replied. "I said I'm staying." He flopped over in his sleeping bag and gave the room his back.

"Okay," said Kate. She sounded about as fed up with the way Ethan was acting as Kyle was. "If you're sure this is what you want. We'll need the map so we can find our way."

Ethan let out a beleaguered sigh as he sat up, rummaged through his pack, and practically threw the map at Kate.

"Thank you." Kate picked up the map from the floor where it had landed, and put it in her own backpack. Then she stormed out of the house.

Mary glanced at Ethan before following Kate outside.

Kyle knew Kate was mad at Ethan, but he didn't like seeing them fight like this. For all any of them knew, this might be the last time they saw Ethan. He didn't want Kate feeling regretful because of a stupid fight. But he didn't know what else to do.

"I hope you'll change your mind." Kyle waited for a response.

Nothing.

Cat hopped off the couch and joined them. Like Mary, Cat took one more look at Ethan before heading outside.

Kyle didn't want to leave with this fight causing so much anger between them. He turned back to talk to Ethan, but Ethan rolled onto his side away from Kyle and pulled the bag over his head.

Message received.

# CHAPTER TWENTY-SEVEN

Kyle hated leaving Ethan behind, but maybe he was safer staying with the old guard instead of coming on the journey with the group. They had no idea what was ahead of them.

If Ethan turned out to be the only surviver of the group, at least he knew how to get home and tell everyone there what happened.

Besides, Kyle was tired of Ethan acting like such a spoiled kid. When he asked the old guard why he hadn't received a gift as well was beyond selfish. He'd acted like the jealous kid at his best friend's birthday party.

Kyle couldn't deny that he wouldn't mind the break from having to hold his punches around Ethan. Literal punches.

But it still bothered him that the team had split up. How was he going to keep everyone safe in different places?

The three moons of Terra lit up the streets of the kingdom and made it easier for them to travel. The moons were beautiful, but Kyle missed his world where there was only one.

"What now?" Kate asked. Kyle could tell she was asking in order to keep her mind from thinking about leaving Ethan behind. Kate was very protective of Ethan, so Kyle was beyond surprised that she had given in so easily.

Maybe Kate was Ethan-exhausted, too?

"We head for the forest," Kyle replied, but in truth, he had no idea which direction to go.

"It's this way," said cat. It started off in the exact opposite direction Kyle would have taken them.

"Lead the way." Kyle was relieved he didn't have to take the lead for once. He felt too distracted thinking about Ethan to be making any important decisions.

Cat led them through the streets of the city, and no one said anything for several minutes. Kyle figured they were all thinking about Ethan. They weren't a complete group without him. Even when he was acting like a total jerk.

He was wondering if they should go back, knock Ethan out and drag him along when Kate broke through his thoughts.

"Are we sure leaving Ethan behind was the right thing?" Kate's doubts were feeding Kyle's.

"I hope so," Kyle finally said. What else could he say? He didn't think it was a good idea at all, but Ethan hadn't left them much choice.

They reached the edge of a forest. This one was almost directly opposite on the map from the forest they had taken to get to Kendo Kingdom. There were thick trees and bushes making it almost impossible to see inside, in spite of the the light from the moons.

"It's this way," said Cat, who continued into the forest as if it had super cat vision.

They entered in single file. Kyle felt the noticeable absence of Ethan, and almost turned around to go back for him. But he had to respect Ethan's wishes, however juvenile they appeared to the rest of the group.

He felt like he was missing one of his arms without Ethan, but he would have to get used to it. He knew they would probably end up going in different directions for college, but that was still two years away.

Kyle tried to convince himself it was better for Ethan to stay with the guard. He was safer in the Kendo Kingdom. They would find the flowers, bring them back, break the spell, and by then Ethan would have figured out how to get them home.

The sun had risen and was slowly clearing the darkness from the forest. They continued to trek their way through branches and vines, despite there being no sign of a trail or path. Cat seemed to know where it was going though, so they all followed.

In silence.

When they finally came out of the forest into a clearing, the sun was almost full in the sky. They had to have been walking for hours. Lost in his thoughts, it had felt more like only a few minutes.

He could see snow-capped mountains ahead in the distance.

There was a large cascading waterfall through the middle of one range. He squinted his eyes to check out the waterfall more carefully. It was flowing down as it should be, which was a huge relief.

"We've been walking so long," Mary said. "I need to rest." As if to prove her point, she shucked off her backpack and all but collapsed where she had been standing.

"Good idea." Kyle finally began to feel the effects of their long walk, and agreed with Mary. Sitting down for a few minutes wouldn't be a bad thing. "Let's stop here."

He sat down next to Mary, and Kate joined them. They each rummaged through their backpacks for something to eat.

It was a surprise to Kyle that they kept finding food in their backpacks. Was it Spirit Neal constantly restocking their food supply? The old guard hadn't offered them food, and yet their backpacks never ran out.

"Cat, do you have a name other than Cat?" Mary asked, as she shared some of her cheese with the feline.

Cat munched on the cheese before responding. "What is a name?"

"It's what your parents give you." Mary replied.

Kyle thought it was a little more complicated than that, but wasn't going to contradict Mary. The group had already had enough unimportant arguments that hadn't gone so well.

"No," said Cat. "We just know each other by the way we look."

"Hmmm," Mary said, and Kyle could see from the look on her face that she was considering something very serious. "How about Lucky?"

"What does Lucky mean?" asked Cat, as he moved closer to Mary and sat next to her.

"It means…" She paused and scrunched up her face, considering. "Well, it means someone who is very fortunate. Things seem to always go your way."

"Lucky," replied Cat, rolling the word around. "I like that. I have a human name."

He ran around in circles, prancing between Mary and Kate. "My name is Lucky," he said to Kate, as if she hadn't been sitting there and heard the entire conversation. "I'm a part of a human pride."

"He looks happy." Kyle was glad at least one of them was happy. Might as well be the cat.

"He is." Mary smiled fondly at Lucky, but Kyle could tell that she wasn't nearly as happy as the cat.

This whole thing with Ethan had upset all of them. He wished they could go back and replay it all over again with a better ending. But he wasn't sure it would have ended any differently than it had.

"We should get moving." He had to quit second-guessing the argument with Ethan and move on. Literally and figuratively. "We still have a long way to go."

"I'll use the pencil to send us closer to the fire flowers," said a voice from behind them. "That'll cut our travel time."

They all turned around at once, and Kate screamed.

# CHAPTER TWENTY-EIGHT

Ethan stood where they had exited the forest. Kate ran to him and threw her arms around him. Kyle knew Kate had been upset, but didn't know how much until he saw her hugging Ethan.

"Holy cow," Kate said, still hugging Ethan. "You scared the crap out of us. But I'm so glad to see you."

"I'm glad you changed your mind." Mary hugged Ethan when Kate was finished, but Kyle noticed she was shy about it. She acted like she might break something if she hugged too hard.

Kyle was beyond relieved to see him, but he was still pretty angry about the way Ethan had acted. He was torn between hugging him, and punching him.

Didn't Ethan realize out hard this was? Kyle didn't want to set him off again, so he stood back waiting for Ethan to make the first move.

"I'm sorry," said Ethan, and Kyle was relieved.

He could deal with an apology, and was even willing to offer one himself. They had both taken it too far.

Ethan approached Kyle like he too was uncertain if he would be getting a hug or a punch. "I had a nice long chat with the guard after you all left, and I realized -- or more like, he told me -- that I was being kind of a jerk."

"Kind of?" Kyle asked, but he grinned so that Ethan knew he was at least trying to be open.

"I'm sorry about my dumb attitude." Ethan spoke to the ground, but Kyle knew it was meant for him. "I know you are only trying to keep us all together. But sometimes I feel useless. Like you don't need me."

"Need you?" Kate gasped, and Kyle thought she was going to be the one to start swinging. "Who do you think is going to get us back home? Me? Mary? Kyle? Do we know how to fix that thing on your wrist? No, we don't. You do. You are the brains in this outfit."

Kyle flinched. He knew Ethan was ten times smarter than he was, but it still stabbed to hear Kate say it out loud.

"But I'm also the one who landed us here in the first place." Ethan hung his head, and Kyle could see that this was the real problem. Ethan felt guilty for stranding them in this place, and he hadn't been able to get them back home yet.

"Ethan." Kyle spoke gently like he was trying to calm a wounded animal. "We all decided to do this together. It wasn't your fault something went wrong. You certainly didn't plan a thunder storm to happen in the middle of our transmission, or whatever."

"I don't know how to get us back home."

"We know you will figure it out." Mary came up to Ethan and laid her hand on his arm.

"We trust you, Ethan," Kyle said. "We always do. Friends together. Friends forever. Right?"

"Right." Ethan looked up and around at the group.

Kyle put his hand out first, and they all stacked hands like they were in a football huddle.

"Friends together. Friends forever." They all chanted it together, and shook their of hands before breaking apart.

"What about me?" asked Lucky.

"You, too, Cat." Ethan bent down and rubbed Lucky's head. "His name is Lucky now," Mary said, and she looked proud of her part in the naming.

"Okay, so a lot has happened since I've been gone." Ethan shook his head in bewilderment, but smiled.

"You said something about a pencil when you arrived?" Kate asked, prompting them to get back on track.

"Right, yes, that's how I was able to get here so quickly." Ethan reached into his backpack and took out the pencil he had found on the balloon ship. "This can take us to the fire flowers much faster than walking."

"See? I knew you were good for something." Kyle laughed as Ethan gently punched him in the shoulder.

"Lucky, you'd better stay close to me." Mary gathered Lucky up into her arms so he wouldn't be left behind.

Then she reached out and took Kyle's left hand. In turn, Kyle took Kate's left hand with his right one. Kate reached out and took Ethan's left hand, leaving his right one free to write.

Ethan wrote large letters in the air as he spoke the words at the same time, "Take us to the fire flowers."

Kyle felt a sharp tug, but he didn't let go of either Mary's or Kate's hands.

His heart skipped a beat and he felt a moment of panic as they were all pulled into nothingness.

# CHAPTER TWENTY-NINE

They landed in exactly the same arrangement, but in a completely different place. It was as if some giant hand had scooped them up and put them right back down again with different scenery.

"Are we near the fire flowers?" Kate asked. "I don't see anything that looks like it could be a flower on fire."

Kyle had been thinking the same thing as he took in the area. The tall trees and colorful foliage made the forest cool and inviting. But Kate was right, He didn't see anything that looked like fire flowers either. Did the pencil take them to the wrong place?

"The fire flowers are heavily guarded," said Lucky, "with soldiers and with King Warren's magic. This is as close at the pencil could take us."

"Guess we're walking from here," said Kate.

"Great, more walking." Ethan groaned.

Kyle opened his mouth to point out that Ethan's magic pencil had cut his walking time in half of what they had all done already. He decided to let it go, and ignore Ethan's whining instead.

Ethan would get with the program, he always did. Except for this morning, but that was a one-off. Everyone was allowed one one-off.

The path they had landed on was wide enough to walk two-by-two. It was nothing like the last forest they'd waded through where they'd had to make their own path.

Kate took the lead for a change, with Mary and Cat in the middle. Kyle was glad to be walking side-by-side with Ethan.

They had already said everything that had needed to be said, and Kyle was glad they could walk companionably again.

It was enough for now to have Ethan with them again. It was enough to hang out and listen to Mary and Lucky talk about inconsequential things.

"Do you have a family?" Mary asked Lucky. "What is a family?" Lucky sounded puzzled, but interested. Kyle thought that was fairly remarkable for a cat.

He'd never thought cats cared much about anything but themselves.

"How do I explain it?" Mary seemed momentarily stumped, and Kyle couldn't blame her. How do you describe a family in a way a cat would understand? "A family is made up of a group of people all related like a mother, a dad and their kids."

Like her name explanation, this was a very limited, not to mention stereotypical, definition for a family. "Family" meant different things to different people. Kyle considered their group his family, even though they weren't related by blood.

"You mean a pride?" Lucky stopped in his tracks. "I have a pride." He sat on his rump, and extended his arms as far as they would go. "It's this big."

Kyle snorted a laugh, then covered it with a cough. He didn't want to offend the cat, but he couldn't help himself. Lucky's arms didn't stretch all that far.

"Wow that's a big pride." Mary was much better at hiding her reaction than he'd been.

"Are they the pride you come from?" Lucky gestured his head toward Kyle and Ethan. He didn't sound very impressed. Maybe Kyle hadn't been as successful covering his laugh as he'd thought.

"Oh, no," Mary replied, shaking her head. Kyle was offended that she seemed so adamant about them not being included in her inner circle. So much for family. "My original pride is back home where we come from.

"Are there any like me where you come from?"

"Yes lots of cats." Mary smiled down at Lucky. "But they usually don't talk. You're my first taking cat."

"I would like to see that one day."

"I'm sure you'd fit in just fine." Mary paused, as if considering her next words. "Can I ask you a personal question?"

"What is personal?"

Again, Kyle covered his laugh. He was starting to like this cat. He was like a four-year-old toddler asking his parents all kinds of annoying questions. It was hilarious to watch. But Mary was taking it all very seriously, with much more patience than Kyle would have had.

Mary would make an excellent teacher. She would need to expand on some of her definitions for things, but she was great at the encouragement part.

"Personal means things only you know that are unique to you." Mary was getting much better with her answers.

"You can ask me anything, Maarry."

"How do you know humans so well?" Mary asked, and Kyle was curious to know the answer to that as well.

"When I was a cub I grew up in the old guard's home with my dam and the others in the pride--" Lucky began.

"Ahhh, I wondered about that," Mary said, and smiled at Lucky. "I kind of figured since you were so familiar with his house."

Lucky nodded, and continued his story. "Our dam used to go hunting and leave us in the human's care. He spoke to us a lot and I just kind of picked it up. When we were older our dam took us on hunting trips and taught us how to catch mice and birds."

"You must be really good at it," said Mary.

"I'm the best." Lucky puffed his chest out with pride. "Are you together now? Are they part of your pride?" Mary asked.

"No. Once we we're old enough to catch our own food, our dam left and never came back." Lucky didn't sound upset, but Kyle couldn't see how the mom leaving wouldn't have left a hole for a kid. Even a cat.

"That's sad, I'm so sorry." Mary glanced down at Lucky. "It is okay," he replied. "It is hard sometimes, but I can catch my own meals and find shelter when I need it. It is our nature and that is our way."

"I never realized a cat's life is so hard." Mary sounded deflated. Kyle was one hundred percent certain that when they returned home, Mary was going to be adopting a whole pride of cats.

"It is not so bad," continued Lucky. "I found a new pride and life just got better."

"You mean we're your pride now?" Mary giggled, but Kyle knew there would be no getting rid of Lucky.

"Yes." Lucky glanced up at Mary, and seemed less sure of himself. "Don't you like Lucky?"

"Yes, I like Lucky a lot." Mary beamed a smile down on the cat.

"Does he like me?" Lucky gestured his head back in Kyle's direction.

Kyle quickly looked away, pretending he hadn't been listening to the entire conversation.

"Kyle?" Mary asked, even though she knew who the cat had pointed to. "Yes he does."

Kyle would have liked to have been asked himself, but he let Mary handle it. Lucky seemed to be her cat after all.

"And the others?"

Was the cat fishing for compliments? Or did he really care about whether or not they liked him? Kyle had never met a more insecure cat.

"Yes they do, too. We all like you, Lucky." Mary was more assuring than Kyle would have been.

"Then I will stay with my new pride." Lucky made the announcement like it was his choice.

Kyle would never throw a cat out into the cold, but still he felt a prickle of annoyance that the humans hadn't even been consulted. What if one of them had been allergic to cats?

Mary bent down and scratched Lucky on his head, and Kyle knew that had sealed the decision.

They were the proud new owners of Lucky the Cat.

# CHAPTER THIRTY

"Not another freakin' forest." Kyle was getting really tired of traipsing through one forest after another. Did this land have nothing but forests to connect the towns?

Directly ahead of them was yet another forest. The only remarkable difference with this one was that it had glowing arrows on the trees.

Although, when he stopped being grumpy, and truly looked around, he could see that this one also had incredible neon and translucent flowers, plants and bushes. Even the butterflies glowed. So, that was new.

"What is this place?" Kate asked, as she turned around in a circle taking everything in.

"It's beautiful," said Mary, who also seemed to be impressed.

"It reminds me of an amusement park I used to go to." Kyle remembered this old-time amusement park his parents used to take him to when he was about five or six years old. He hadn't been old enough (or tall enough) to ride the really big rides, but the little rides all lit up and glowed when he rode them. Exactly like this forest.

Kate reached out to touch one of the plants, but Lucky jumped in front of her, almost tripping her.

"Don't touch that." He wound through her legs, distracting her from the plants. "They are full of evil magic, one touch --"

He was interrupted when a deer ran down the path, startling everyone. The deer saw them and panicked, veering off the path and inadvertently touching one of the plants.

The group watched in horror as the deer turned into one of the plants.

"That happens," said the cat, as if this was something he saw on a regular basis. They all stared at him in shock. "As long as you stay on the path and away from the plants you'll be okay."

Kyle wanted to kick himself for letting his guard down. This wasn't the amusement park with his parents where he was safe. This was a crazy world they didn't know anything about. This was a world with talking cats, two-headed monsters, and beautiful but poisonous flowers.

Here, he could be turned into stone or a plant with one wrong move. Actually, he was wrong. This was an amusement park alright. Just not the fun kind.

His angry thoughts were broken when he heard something big coming toward them on the path. Whatever it was, he was already prepared for it not to be friendly.

"Oh man, now what?" Ethan sounded as if he'd reached his stress capacity as well.

"Get ready." Kyle pulled out his sword and stood ready to fight whatever came through the bushes. As if he'd given a signal, everyone else drew their weapons, too.

"Nothing happens." Kate shook her sword, apparently expecting that to help turn it on. If they hadn't been in eminent danger, Kyle would have thought it immensely funny.

"Your weapons only work in battle." Lucky sounded awfully nonchalant considering Kyle was pretty sure they were all going to be squashed in a stampede.

A ten foot tall, massively hairy beast emerged from the bushes. It looked like some kind of giant plant, but with claws. Its eyes were red and it growled like an angry bear. And it was closing in on them fast.

"Mine works," Mary said, and she stood in ready position like she had been practicing all her life.

She grabbed her archer's bow and pulled on the string. An arrow appeared instantly and she let it fly. It missed the target and exploded in the forest. She tried again, pulling the bow and shooting the arrow that magically appeared. But she and missed again.

The bear-plant-thing was getting closer. It was too big to fight.

"Run!" Kyle shouted. They had to get away from it.

Mary continued to fire her bow while running, but none of the arrows hit the target. They ran down the path as fast as they could, trying to leave the charging creature behind.

The path ended abruptly with nothing but the glowing plants all around them. And the creature was still charging toward them.

Mary made another attempt firing an arrow and finally hit the creature. The arrow exploded on impact.

"I got him," Mary shouted, and started jumping up and down with excitement.

Kyle watched in disbelief as the bear-plant creature shook off the flaming arrow and roared. He was still coming for them, and he was even more angry.

"Get us out of here, Ethan!" Kate screamed at the top of her lungs.

Ethan pulled out the pencil and spoke the words as he wrote in the sky. "Take us to the fire flowers. Now."

They all grabbed each others hands and once again Kyle felt a sharp tug just as he saw the creature swing out at them with his sharp claws.

# CHAPTER THIRTY-ONE

When he opened his eyes, Kyle was unsurprised to see they were standing, yet again, at another forest. It made him want to scream.

Does this stupid planet have nothing but forests? Why couldn't they land next to a lovely, peaceful, green valley? Something with gentle slops and a babbling river. What was with all these forests that got weirder and weirder the more they traveled?

This forest consisted of strangely misshapen trees, all in purples, oranges, browns and grays. It looked like something out of a Dr. Seuss book. Definitely not the natural colors of the forests on Earth.

The trees grew so high they blocked out the natural light trying to get inside. It was too dark, and too quiet. The whole thing was giving Kyle the creeps.

"Where are we?" Kyle didn't expect an answer from anyone, knowing they all must be as confused as he was.

"Is this the Kendo Kingdom forest?" Mary asked Lucky. "This just won't do," muttered the cat in return. "No no not at all." He wasn't paying any attention to the group, and he was wandering around in circles, very agitated.

"I don't see anything that looks like fire flowers." Ethan glanced around, then looked pointedly at the pencil.

Kyle felt hysterical laughter bubbling up in his chest.

What did Ethan think? That the pencil was going to talk to him? Or that maybe he could use an eraser and take them back to where they were before? Ethan examined the pencil like it had answers. Kyle knew, even in this place, that was impossible.

"Lucky?" Mary asked. "What's wrong?"

"We have to go," Lucky said. "We can't stay here." He began pacing, as if expecting to find an escape route.

"Why? What's wrong?" Mary stood in the path of the cat, forcing him to stop and talk.

"This place is bad." Lucky looked nervous, which Kyle had never seen a cat do before. "Even I don't come here. This is the forest of Queen Evilya."

"Who is Queen Evilya?" asked Kate.

"She controls this part of the woods," said Lucky. "She is very mean and very angry."

"Does she have an army?" Kyle didn't want to have to fight an army. Especially if the ruler of that army was mean and angry.

"No," replied Lucky. "It is just her.

"Then it should be a piece of cake." Kate pulled her sword and practiced a few moves. Kyle could see that she was getting better with it, and he couldn't help but feel happy for her. There wasn't much that Kate couldn't do when she wanted it badly enough.

"She controls these woods," continued Lucky, which made Kyle wonder about the mind of someone who controlled crazy trees like these. "She can make the forest do things. And when she catches you she eats you."

Kyle rolled his eyes. More creatures that wanted to eat humans. It wasn't that he didn't believe the cat. It was just that Kyle was beginning to wonder how anyone survived on this planet at all.

"That's our cue to go then." Ethan raised the pencil and spoke the words as he wrote them in the air, "Take us to the fire flowers."

The all grabbed each other's hands once again, and Kyle closed his eyes waiting for the now familiar tug.

Nothing happened. He didn't feel a tug. He opened his eyes to see they were still in the creepy forest. "What happened?"

"I don't know," Ethan said, then shrugged. "It should have worked."

Ethan raised the pencil again, then spoke the words as he wrote a new message. "Take us back to Kendo Kingdom."

Again, Kyle waited for the familiar tug. Still nothing happened.

"Your magic doesn't work here." Lucky sat in the circle of the group and glared at them as if they were all idiots. "There are only two ways out. Walk out. Or die."

Kyle had never wanted to kick a cat before, but this one made him crazy. He could have told them the rules before they'd started trying to use the pencil. What a waste of time. A potentially dangerous waste of time.

"So, if we can't use magic," said Kate, speaking in a matter of fact tone, "then we'll just have to be real careful."

"We have no choice," said Kyle, feeling grumpy. She made it sound like they hadn't been being careful all along. "Let's get out of here." At least they don't have to go into that creepy forest.

They took the clearing with the giant colorful flowers instead, and Kyle felt a little bit better about their direction.

"Wow," remarked Kate. "Those look so beautiful."

Kyle wondered if the evil queen would notice if they picked a couple to take back with them. Maybe she took inventory of all of her flowers while she was controlling her forest. It would probably be bad to pick any.

"Yeah let's take a closer look." Mary started for the flowers, but the cat cut her off and she almost tripped over him.

"I don't think it is a good idea, Maarry." Lucky looked adamant, but Mary ignored him by stepping over him. "We should go," he said to her retreating back.

As they got closer to the flowers, the buds opened up.

Inside each flower was what looked like comfortable beds.

A mist floated out of each flower, and covered the group.

It smelled like home to Kyle. It smelled like the iced sugar cookies his mom used bake for him when he was stressed about taking a test, or an important paper was due. The scent was so overwhelming, and made him so lonely for home, he wanted to curl up and stay here for ever.

"Smell that," Kate said, and she sounded wistful. "It smells like the perfume my mom used to wear."

"It smells wonderful," said Mary. "It smells like a brand new book." Her voice trailed off, and her eyes started to droop. Through a yawn she said, "I don't know why, but I'm so tired all of a sudden."

"Me too," said Ethan, and he yawned even louder than Mary. "Those buds look so comfortable."

"They look like beds." Mary climbed into the flower, and crawled into the bed.

"No, Maarry no." Lucky screamed at her, but she didn't seem to hear him.

"They do look comfortable." Despite their appearance, Kyle still felt unsure about climbing into one of those things. Their scent was so comforting though.

"I could use a nap." Kate, yawning, crawled into one of the other bed flowers.

"No it's a trick! Don't go! Meow! Meow, Meow, Meooooow!" Lucky was frantic, but Kyle didn't understand what he was so concerned about. They could all certainly use a rest. They had been traveling all day. And this place felt so safe and welcoming.

"We have to keep going." The cat was still screaming at them. "We have to get away. You can't go to sleep here. You'll die if you do!"

"Not now Lucky." Mary sounded as if she couldn't stay awake any longer. "I'm just going to take a little nap."

Ethan must have agreed with Mary and Kate, because he flopped into the nearest bed flower, and was fast asleep before his head hit the pillow.

Kyle still felt something nagging at the back of his mind, but couldn't sort it out. Besides the cat's screeching was giving him a headache. It was definitely time for a nap.

He went to the bed flower that smelled the most like cookies, crawled inside and collapsed on the bed. It was the most comfortable bed he'd ever slept in. So much better than sleeping on the floor in a sleeping bag.

The last thing he saw as his eyelids drooped was the flower closing around him. It was infinitely peaceful. And the outside world with all of it's necessary decisions ceased to exist.

# CHAPTER THIRTY-TWO

Kyle sat on the bench in the locker room, still in his football gear. He was too upset with himself to even remove his shoulder pads. He kept playing the game over in his mind.

He was supposed to be the best. How could he have made such a stupid rookie mistake like that?

"Hey buddy, what's up?" Ethan stood in front of him. Kyle hadn't even noticed him. It was like he'd appeared out of nowhere.

"Where'd you come from?" Kyle couldn't remember if Ethan had been there the whole time. Or if he'd come up within the last few seconds of Kyle beating himself up.

"Don't worry about that man," said Ethan, attempting to soothe. "Everything's cool."

Cool? Since when did Ethan say, "Cool?" Something was off about him, but Kyle couldn't place it.

"Wait a minute." Kyle sat up straighter and took in the room. "How did I get here. The last thing I remember..."

What did he remember? It seemed important. He didn't remember actually playing the football game. That was really weird.

Where was Kate? He had been with Kate. He definitely remembered that part. Something was very off about this.

"Everything's fine," said Ethan again. "You're here, I'm here, everything's just cool now."

There's that word again. Kyle has never heard Ethan talk like this before.

Ethan opened his arms and tried to hug Kyle, and Kyle knew that was wrong. Ethan was not a hugger.

"You're not Ethan." Kyle shook off the impostor-Ethan and stood up. "Who are you?"

"Sure I'm Ethan," Impostor Ethan responded, his voice so full of fake insincerity Kyle wanted to shake him. "Who else would I be?"

Impostor Ethan's face disappeared, and Kyle almost screamed. He knew this thing wasn't his friend, Ethan, but it was still frightening to see him without a face. Nothing was there on the front of his head but smooth emptiness.

The faceless Impostor Ethan again tried to hug Kyle, and this time he succeeded. Kyle screamed, "Get off me!"

But the faceless Impostor Ethan had him in a vice grip.

Kyle punched and kicked struggling to get free. He broke away from the thing and tried to run. His legs were leaden, and his feet kept sticking to the floor.

"What's happening to me?" Kyle couldn't move, and that thing kept coming for him. Even his arms felt paralyzed.

"It's alright." The faceless Impostor Ethan put his arms around Kyle again. "I'm here now."

Kyle kept struggling, his fear ratcheting up to full-blown panic mode. He managed to break free one more time, when the whole locker room morphed into the dojo area at his high school.

The Sensei and Kyle were dressed in their martial arts Gi with five other students divided into three groups of twos.

"Ready," barked Sensei.

Everyone moved to first position, and they bowed to each other.

"Fight," shouted Sensei.

While the others sized-up each other, Kyle moved like a pro. He looked for weakness in his opponent's movements. His style was to let the opponent get in a few jabs so he could study his training. Kyle blocked the jabs with little effort.

Then Kyle saw his opening and made his move. His feet and fists flew, faster than even Kyle imagined. But for every swing he made his opponent blocked in defense.

His opponent was better. He landed one, sometimes two, punches for every one of Kyle's.

Kyle's confidence faded as he found himself on the defensive. His opponent kept attacking, his blows hitting their mark every time.

Kyle's strength faded quickly, and he fell.

"Stop." Sensei's voice rang out in the dojo. Everyone stopped fighting and returned back to first position.

Sensei moved between the rows as if inspecting his troops. "You are all my best students," he said, "but you can do better. At best I should see a draw between all of you.

Kyle you are better than this. Stop holding back and fight."

Sensei stood in front of Kyle and glared at him. Kyle felt immediately inadequate. He was better than this. How could he have let his opponent get in so many punches?

"I'm trying, Sensei." Kyle started to explain, but he felt so defeated. "I don't know --"

"No." Sensei cut him off emphatically. "You're not trying, and you do know." Sensei poked Kyle in the chest above his heart. "Gather your chi and envision your victory. It's in you, Kyle. Only you can unleash the fury. Do you understand what I am saying?"

"Yes, Sensei, I understand," Kyle replied, more out of reflex than understanding.

"Then show me." Sensei moved back to his position to watch. "Ready," he said again.

The group again faced each other and got ready to fight. Kyle faced his opponent, but this time it was Ethan. When had Ethan shown up?

"Fight," shouted Sensei, and Kyle didn't have any more time to think about it.

"You know this is a waste of time. Right?" Ethan circled, and Kyle watched him for clues to his fighting technique.

"No, it's not." Kyle was trying to ignore what Ethan was saying, and focus on the fight. He knew Ethan was trying to throw him off mentally, so that he could be defeated physically.

"But you can't win, and you know it." Ethan grinned smugly at Kyle.

"You're wrong," Kyle said. "Sensei is right."

"No," said Ethan. But this time he was frustrated, no longer smug. "Listen to me and stop struggling. I'm here now and everything is okay."


Kyle knew he was succeeding against Ethan. Ethan was angry that Kyle wouldn't give in so easily, and he knew that was going to make Ethan lose.

Ethan must have come to the same conclusion, because all of a sudden his face disappeared.

"Get away from me," Kyle screamed. He looked around the dojo, and nothing seemed familiar to him. "Where Am I?"

Kyle felt a stinging in his leg, and knew that Ethan landed a strike.

Ethan had stabbed him.

# CHAPTER THIRTY-THREE

Kyle jerked awake but was disoriented. He fought the urge to go back to sleep, but he was not going to go through one more of those nightmares. He couldn't remember where he was, but he could see that he was held fast by large vines all wrapped around him.

He felt his surge of adrenaline from the nightmare slowing down, and wanted to go back to sleep. But he knew that if he stayed inside the pod-thing, it would eventually suck the life out of him. He had to get out.

"Can anybody hear me?" He shouted, hoping one of his friends could hear him and help.

The cat's face appeared through a crack in the vines holding Kyle's pod closed. "You have to get out and help the others."

"I think I've been stabbed in the leg." Kyle was confused, but he remembered being stabbed. His leg must be gushing blood. What if he lost consciousness from blood loss? The plant would eat him for sure.

"You weren't stabbed," replied Lucky. "I bit you to wake you up. You are fine."

Kyle felt stupid. He wouldn't die of blood loss from a cat bite. He just hoped the thing didn't have rabies.

"Hey, what?" Ethan sounded groggy, but he must have heard Kyle yelling. "What is this? I can't get out."

"Ethan, we have to get out," Kyle shouted. He didn't hear anything again from Ethan, and was afraid he had gone back to sleep.

"We have to get out of here," shouted Lucky at Kyle as if worried he'd go back to sleep again.

Kyle struggled to get out of his bud, but was completely bound by the vines and he couldn't get lose. He needed something sharp to slice through the vines. Would the cat's teeth be able to chew through them?

He was also struggling to stay conscious. His mind was foggy, and he couldn't think clearly. Why did he need something sharp again?

Sharp. Cut the vines. Cat teeth? No, a knife was sharp. "Lucky," Kyle yelled, his mind clear for a moment. "I need my sword."

Lucky disappeared from the gap and Kyle heard rustling outside the pod. A moment later, the cat was back and shoving Kyle's sword in through the gap. Kyle couldn't reach up far enough to grab it.

"Drop it by my hand." If the cat's aim was good, Kyle would be able to reach the sword and cut one of his hands free. Then he would be able to free himself before clearing out the others from their pods.

Lucky's aim was perfect. Kyle sliced through his bonds and took aim to stab through the pod. He had a moment's thought for the pod as a living being, but immediately quashed it. This thing had been ready to eat him.

He stabbed through the bottom of the pod and fell to the ground. With a few more easy slices through vines and pods, he was able to free the others.

They were all groggy from their drug-induced slumbers, but the fresh air easily brought them all back to their senses.

"We have to go now before Queen Evilya comes." Lucky, clearly agitated, bounced back and forth between each member of the group. "No one likes her, not even King Warren. She loved him once, but when she found out that he loved the princess instead, she betrayed him. That's why he banished her to this realm forever. Now her heart is dark and evil. We have to go now."

That was the most Kyle had ever heard from the cat, and it all came out in a rush. Lucky must really be scared. That was all the proof Kyle needed. It was time to go.

"I agree with Lucky," said Mary, as if they needed to vote.

"Let's go." Kate agreed, and moved to pick up her backpack, which had fallen when she entered the pod.

Kyle stooped to retrieve his own backpack, then had to take a step back when a large tree stump began to change shape. He knew this was a magical world, but tree stumps didn't usually move like that.

It finally morphed into a beautiful royal chair. In the chair sat a woman who looked exactly like Kyle's girlfriend.

"Lynn?" Kyle was stupefied. How was it possible that Lynn was in this world with them? Was his brain still foggy from the sleeping mist of the pods?

"Who dares enter my Kingdom without my permission?" The Lynn look-alike pounded her scepter into the ground, and the forest shook.

She certainly got mad quickly like Lynn.

"We're here by mistake." Kyle tried to explain without getting them killed. "We didn't mean to trespass."

"Do not lie to the Queen," shouted the Lynn look-alike, although Kyle was certain she wasn't Lynn anymore than the old guard had been Mr. Aaron. "It's impossible to come here without magic."

"We're very sorry," Kyle said in what he hoped was a soothing tone. "We'll leave and never come back."

"Tell me what magic brought you here," demanded the Queen, "or no one will leave here alive."

Kyle was strangely calm. Maybe it was all the practice he had with the actual Lynn, who could be very explosive when she was angry. He felt calmly capable of soothing this angry Queen. He watched her, waiting for her to get it all off her chest. He'd learned with Lynn that all she really needed was to be heard.

"How dare you use your feeble magic in my kingdom." Again, she pounded her scepter, as if she were a judge and they were on trial. The ground shook again.

"This won't be good." Ethan had come up next to Kyle, and whispered in his ear.

"Get ready," Kyle whispered back.

The earth shook again and the leaves lying on the ground shot into the air. They hovered above the group then changed into leaf shaped daggers.

Daggers flew toward the group, and Kyle used his sword to deflect them. Kate expertly unsheathed her sword and stepped up to help Kyle.

When there are no more flying dagger leaves, Kyle took a breath and smiled at Kate, who smiled back. They had done it.

His joy of winning was short-lived, however, when he saw the tigers advancing on them.

Ethan tried blinding them with his crystal ball but they keep advancing.

Lucky lunged at the tigers biting and throwing them to the ground. Kyle was impressed. He had no idea the cat could take on tigers like that. He would have to be careful not to make the cat angry in the future.

Tree roots came up from out the ground and grabbed their legs.

"We have to get out of here," Ethan shouted through the noise, struggling to get loose from the roots.

"We can't fight her without the magic," Kate said, as she slashed at the roots binding her legs to free herself. Then she cut Ethan free from his root prison.

Kyle cut his bindings, and then freed Mary. "Run for it," he shouted, and they all ran for the woods.

"Come back here," the Queen bellowed, "I command it!"

Kyle wouldn't let the group stop no matter how much that evil queen looked like Lynn.

# CHAPTER THIRTY-FOUR

Kyle was breathing heavy by the time they reached the clearing. He was in great shape from football, but he had never run that hard before in his life.

"Did she follow us?" Kyle asked through his gasping. He was afraid to look around and check for himself. If she'd followed, they were all going to die because his energy was completely spent.

"No," Ethan responded, after taking a quick look behind them. I wonder why."

"She can't," said Lucky. He didn't sound nearly as winded as the rest of them. But then, he was a cat. "She's not permitted outside of her realm."

"How do you know so much about this place?" Mary sounded suspicious, and Kyle wondered what had changed her mind about trusting the cat as she had before. "Have you been here before?"

"No," replied the cat, and he tilted his head at Mary as if also wondering about her tone. "But others have and they told me many things."

Kyle scanned the clearing wondering what other crazy magical fate was waiting for them. It appeared far too quiet. Which meant that it couldn't possibly be as peaceful as it seemed. He hated being so pessimistic, but it was probably the only thing keeping them safe.

"How much you wanna bet there's another trap over there?" Apparently Kate felt the same way Kyle did, and he didn't know whether to laugh or shake his head.

"I'm not taking that bet. I'm sure of it," said Kyle, then he sighed. "Unfortunately, we don't have another choice. We already know what's behind us, and we aren't going back there." He gestured back to where the evil queen was. "Keep your eyes open."

They proceeded cautiously into the clearing. The minute they stepped foot onto the green grass, soldiers appeared on the other side. They lined up with catapults already loaded with fire boulders.

The sky instantly went gray and gloomy, but the clearing in front of them was still a beautiful green field. Kyle was overwhelmed by an incredible sense of deja vu.

Then he saw the man on the large black horse wearing robes and had a flowing gray beard. He knew the man. He also knew the man was not a good man.

The man was King Warren.

I remember this in my dream," Kyle said. He felt like he was outside of himself, watching this play out all over again. "They were expecting us."

"How'd they know?" Ethan asked Kyle, looking very confused.

"I don't know." Kyle didn't have answers for Ethan. He didn't even have answers for himself.

"A spy?" asked Kate, which seemed like the logical conclusion. But still, Kyle didn't know.

"Who?" asked Mary. "It wasn't any of us."

"I'm beginning to wonder," said Kate, who looked pointedly at the cat.

Lucky appeared confused, but Kyle wasn't buying it. Kyle was siding with Kate.

"No," said Mary, moving closer to the cat as if to shield him. "It wasn't him, he wouldn't do that to us."

Mary was always too easy to trust. Usually Kyle found it sweet, but not now when it could get them all killed.

"What is wrong with her, Maarry?" asked Lucky, and Kyle was convinced the cat had drawn out Mary's name on purpose. "Is she mad with me?"

"Who else could have given us away?" Kate glared at Mary, as if willing her to see the logic.

"You're wrong," replied Mary, and she actually stomped her foot for emphasis. "It wasn't him."

The argument would have to wait for another time, because Kyle noticed that King Warren was riding out on his horse.

"Hey," Kyle said in warning. "We have bigger problems right now." He pointed to King Warren entering the clearing.

Lucky's fur rose and his back rounded as he let out a menacing hiss. Apparently King Warren wasn't any friend of the cat. Unless this was an act to throw them off the fact that he was a traitor.

"You came for the fire flowers." King Warren's voice carried across the clearing to them. "Well, you won't get them. But I am impressed that you made it this far. And I'm feeling generous. I will let you live if you leave here now."

His friends all looked at each other, and Kyle was worried that they might actually be considering leaving.

But Mary dissuaded them immediately. "We need our weapons," she said. "Will they work now, Lucky?"

"Yes," replied Lucky, who appeared proud of her. "They will work in battle."

Mary pulled her bow. Kate readied her sword. And Ethan stood with his pencil ready to conjure anything.

Kyle felt another wave of deja vu, remembering his dream.

But he also remembered that these were his friends and they always had each others' backs. He was so proud to be among them.

"We've come a long way," Kyle shouted back to the king. "We're not going back without them!"

Even from this distance, Kyle could see that the king was not pleased by their response. "Then die."

King Warren turned his horse and went back to his line of soldiers. He signaled his men to move their weapons into the clearing.

There were too many men and weapons against the four of them. Kyle grounded himself as he had been taught by Sensei in the dojo, and knew he needed to take command. "We need more help here, Ethan."

Kyle knew from his dream what would happen next, and he stepped closer to Kate and Mary to make room.

# CHAPTER THIRTY-FIVE

"On it." Ethan wrote in the sky and spoke the words out loud, "We need more soldiers."

Fifty large wolves appeared next to Ethan. The wolves were all wearing padded protective gear. Several prides of roaring tigers similarly garbed as the wolves appeared and formed a semi-circle around them all.

"Wow," shouted Ethan, impressed with himself.

"So, what's the plan?" asked Mary, who appeared as calm as Kyle.

"Hit 'em fast and hard." Kyle had heard that in a movie once, and it sounded like it would work.

"Really?" Ethan asked. Ethan must have seen the same movie, because he sounded skeptical. "That's the plan?

Really?"

"You got something better?" Kyle was wide open for other suggestions. He wasn't the kind of leader who pretended to have all the answers. He would definitely take options.

But the group was silent. No one had any come up with other ideas, and King Warren had signaled his first line forward.

"And so it begins," said Kate, as she waived her sword a few times to limber up.

"Take 'em down!" Kyle shouted the battle cry and charged across the clearing. He knew that his magically gifted friends were following behind him. The four-legged animals out-paced them running toward King Warren's army.

King Warren must have heard Kyle's shout because he looked furious. Kyle saw him wave his archers forward to form two front rows.

"Archers! Ready!" The King's shout was heard across the clearing, despite the noise from the advancing wolves and tigers with Kyle.

Kyle expected a volley of arrows to rain down on them, but apparently there was dissension among the ranks, because it didn't happen right away.

"Give the command." The king was yelling at one of his troops.

Kyle assumed it must be a first lieutenant or someone. He wasn't as knowledgeable when it came to actual battles. "Archers! Fire!" shouted the lieutenant-guy.

Kyle shouted a warning to Kate, "Incoming!"

"I got it," Kate replied, and Kyle felt such a wave of admiration for her quick abilities.

Arrows flew from the King's archers spearing several of the animals. But the moment of hesitation from the king's soldier had allowed Kate time to throw her cape around them as a shield.

The arrows bounced off the cape sounding like rain hitting an umbrella, They kept running, advancing on the enemy army.

Kyle heard King Warren yell for a second volley of arrows and worried the cape wouldn't hold as a shield through the second round. He wondered how long Kate would be able to hold it up and fight with her sword at the same time.

Again, arrows rained down on them. And again the four of them were still protected under Kate's shield.

"It's too much." Kate stumbled, but picked herself up again and continued. "I don't know how much longer I can hold it."

Kate was incredible. They all were, but she was pulling a double-shift with the cloak and the sword. He has always known Kate was remarkable, but he was seeing it in full swing.

"Ready the catapults," shouted the king over the battle cries.

Dread spread through Kyle's entire body. They would never be able to withstand stones of fire being hurled at them. Not even Kate's cloak could shield them from that.

Kyle was suddenly hit by a vision that he hadn't remembered being in his dream. He could see exactly where the fire flowers are located. The vision was such a surprise, he stopped dead in his tracks. Mary almost ran into him from behind.

"I know where the fire flowers are." He stopped the others under Kate's cloak. "They're just past his kingdom."

Ethan pulled out his crystal ball, and studied it for a moment. "You're right, but we have to get passed his forces to reach them."

A flaming bomb from one of the enemy catapults landed within a few feet of Kate. Kyle slashed it with his sword and it broke into thousands of tiny icicles, all shattering on the ground.

"We should pull back before it's too late." Mary looked exhausted. The cat had been fighting by her side, but she was running out of energy like the rest of them. "We need another plan."

"We have to try." Kyle wasn't willing to give up. They were too close, and had come too far to give up.

Ethan spoke into his crystal ball and a brilliant bright light poured out of it, blinding the front lines of enemy soldiers. It gave Kyle the opportunity he needed to draw his sword of fire and ice, freezing some of the soldiers and roasting others while they couldn't see.

"We need more troops." Kate was flagging, Kyle could see it in her posture. But she was as determined as he was.

"Keep fighting." All Kyle could do was keep encouraging them. He would need to break through the lines and reach the fire flowers himself. "We can beat them."

More enemy soldiers kept advancing, and Kyle could feel his small group weakening. Even Kate was showing the strain and her battered cape wouldn't hold much longer.

"This ends now!" King Warren's shout reverberated across the clearing. He unsheathed a glinting sword and raised it high into the air. "Let the powers of the sword go fourth and smite my enemies."

The sword started to glow and the sky blackened even darker than before. Lightning flashed through the sky hitting Kate's shield.

Kyle watched in horror as Kate dropped to the ground, and the cape fell, exposing the group to the onslaught. Kyle couldn't move for several seconds, too stunned that Kate was dead.

Then Kate moaned and pulled herself up off the ground.

She raised her sword ready to go another round, and she looked angry. Kyle was so relieved, he almost passed out.

He knew in that moment that he loved Kate. He loved all of them, but he was in love with Kate.

Sadly, he also knew that the middle of a battle was not the time to declare himself. He was helpless to keep up with all the burning boulders crashing down and exploding the earth around their group.

"Everybody run!" Ethan shouted to the group.

But nothing ever happened in their group without an argument.

"So we're running?" Kate challenged her brother, and Kyle felt like laughing. Of course she was the one arguing with him.

"We've done the best we could." Mary agreed with Ethan. "We can't fight them anymore. He's too powerful."

Ethan was right this time, and Kyle knew it. They all needed to run for cover. All of them, except him. He would keep fighting to give them a chance.

A cacophony of roars filled the sky, and Kyle looked up to see platoons of flying dragons descend on King Warren's soldiers.

The lead dragon swooped down and spewed flames on the soldiers closest to their group. Kyle was stunned to see the old guard, dressed in battle gear, riding the large lead dragon.

"For the Royalty," shouted the old guard, his hand raised wielding a massive sword.

The dragon landed next to Kyle with a resounding thud. The old Guard dismounted quickly and the dragon immediately took flight again to join the others in the air. Several soldiers turned and ran to avoid being ripped apart by the sharp talons of the dragons.

"I'm sure happy to see you." Kyle could barely stand, his breathing was so fast.

"I heard of your bravery," said the old Guard, "and we came to help."

A flaming rock went flying by them, and exploded on impact, spraying earth and stone fragments into the air.

Kyle couldn't imagine how word had gotten back to the old guard, but he wasn't about to look a gift horse -- or dragon -- in the mouth.

"I still have one more fight left in this old body." The guard actually smiled at Kyle, as if he was enjoying himself.

"Then let's do this." Kyle gathered his strength once again, and charged into the fight.

"Revenge shall be mine!" roared the guard from behind. Almost immediately soldiers descended on Kyle and the

Guard who wielded his sword with the strength of several men.

Kyle swung his sword slashing and freezing many soldiers while burning others. He kicked and punched his way as he advanced into the thick of the battle.

He saw a bright flash of fur streak past him heading toward the enemy line. Mary came up on his left, shooting arrows and mowing down soldiers. She had definitely improved her aim.

"Lucky is going to sneak past the soldiers, find the fire flowers and bring them back here to us. We'll need to hold the the soldiers here for him to be able to do that."

King Warren, looking as dark as the thunder clouds over their heads, raised his sword again, and shouted over the noise of he battle. "Let the powers of the sword go fourth and smite my enemies!"

"Fight my friends," the guard shouted in encouragement. "We can defeat them." He continued to engage the soldiers using an impressive combination of martial arts and swordsmen skills, cutting down soldiers in his path.

Lightning shot from King Warren's sword into the sky mixing with the black rolling clouds. Sparking rain fell down from the clouds, striking the flying dragons turning them to stone. They dropped from the sky and crashed onto to the field.

The lightening was non-discriminating as it hit anything in its range. Tigers and wolves were turned to stone in mid-leap. Stone soldiers dropped like dominoes, while others retreated in terror. Only a few were left to fight.

The remaining dragons tried hard to evade the bolts of lightning.

"Dragon roar!" The lead dragon who had carried the old guard roared a powerful roar, as the remaining dragons in the sky swerved to evade the bolts of lightening.

"Dragon growl!" Again the lead dragon roared, even louder than before.

He flew high above the clouds then swooped. The other dragons followed him. Two landed beside Ethan and Kate, gesturing them to climb onto their backs. The Lead Dragon landed next to Mary who, having seen Ethan and Kate, climbed on its back without hesitation.

The dragons with their passengers lifted off and soared back toward the sky.

"Where's Kyle?" Kate shouted, and Kyle looked up to see them all safely on the dragons. Now that they were safe, he was ready to go for the fire flowers.

The dragons circled the battlefield, and Kyle tried to wave them off to fly away. He saw another flash of fur, this time streaking in the opposite direction. It was Lucky, heading in the direction of the flying dragons. He had something in his teeth.

Mary's dragon landed within a few inches of the approaching cat, who came to a screeching halt. He quickly collected his nerve, and hopped up with Mary onto the dragon. The dragon lifted off again, but they still didn't fly away.

Kyle knew they had to be searching for him, but they needed to leave with the flowers while they could.

The dragon swooped closer to the battlefield unleashing a torrent of fire, killing several soldiers.

"Kyle," Mary shouted. "Stay there. I'm gonna' pick you up."

But the sky darkened again, and Kyle knew what was coming next. "Look out!" He shouted the warning, and hoped the dragon had quick reflexes.

He watched as Mary's dragon turned out the way just as a bolt of lightning struck.

He felt his legs go numb, and realized that he had been the one struck by the lightening. He was stuck to the ground and couldn't move, just like it had been in the pod nightmare.

His hand went numb and he dropped his sword. Then his arms lost feeling, and he knew he was dying. His last thought was relief that at least his friends were safe.

# CHAPTER THIRTY-SIX

"We have to go back!" Kate was frantic. Kyle had been turned to stone, and they were leaving him. "Mary tell them we have to go back!"

Kate tried to pull on the dragon's neck to get it to turn around. But it either ignored her, or didn't feel her tugging because it kept a steady line behind the dragon Mary rode.

"Please dragon," Mary was crying, which Kate didn't think was going to help their situation, but Mary was a sensitive soul. "We can't leave our friend behind. We have to go back and get him."

"I'm sorry, my lady," replied her dragon, and Kate heard genuine remorse in his voice. "This battle is lost and we have suffered heavily. If we stay we will be as they are."

"Hey!" Ethan shouted from the dragon following Kate's. "Look at your wrist comm it's green. We can go home."

Kate wanted to knock her brother off his dragon. How could he even think about going home when Kyle was still back on that battlefield turned to stone. They had the fire flowers. They could change him back.

"We can't go home without Kyle." Kate was adamant, and she wanted to be sure Ethan knew it. "We have to find a way to save him first."

But the dragons continued to fly onward, and Kate's heart broke.

Flying dragons or not, there was no way she was going to leave Kyle behind.

www.ingramcontent.com/pod-product-compliance
Lightning Source LLC
Chambersburg PA
CBHW050454110726
47899CB00003B/941